P9-ECJ-571

This book is the fourth in Harper & Row's Native American Publishing Program. All profits from this program are set aside in a special fund and used to support projects designed to aid the Native American people.

Other Books in the Program

Seven Arrows, by Heyemeyohsts Storm
Ascending Red Cedar Moon, by Duane Niatum
Winter in the Blood, by James Welch

A bicentennial celebration is going to take place in 1976. We, the hosts, haven't been asked about our involvement. We feel that if this government is expecting to celebrate its two hundredth birthday in our country, they'd better involve us. . . . Unless the conditions change one hundred eighty degrees, it will be our duty and our responsibility to blow out the candles on the two hundredth birthday cake.

—VERNON BELLECOURT, OJIBWA
INTERNATIONAL FIELD DIRECTOR
AMERICAN INDIAN MOVEMENT

INDIANS' SUMMER

a novel by Nasnaga

Harper & Row, Publishers

New York   Evanston   San Francisco   London

Typography and binding design by Deborah Schure.

Drawings by Nasnaga.

INDIANS' SUMMER

Grateful acknowledgement is made to *Penthouse*,
in which Vernon Bellecourt's quote first
appeared. © by Penthouse International Ltd., 1973.

Library of Congress Cataloging in Publication Data
Nasnaga, 1941–
    Indians' summer.
    I. Title.
PZ4.N258In [PS3564.A83]   813'.5'4   74–20816
ISBN 0–06–451510–9

First Edition

*For the Indian People
and
my daughter,
First Star At Morning*

I would like to thank those who helped me in this work: Dr. Donald Worcester, my teacher; Jacquelyn Skinner, "Warms My Heart," my toughest critic; Douglas Latimer, who made it possible; Mr. and Mrs. M. W. Jones, for their understanding and help; and all those who believe in our people. I wish you peace.

—NASNAGA

Glossary

I have used a few words in this book that probably won't be familiar to many readers. Here are those words and my definitions of them.

Akwesasne: The Mohawk name for their reservation, officially known as St. Regis, which spans the St. Lawrence River in the United States and Canada.

Anishinabe: An Algonkian word meaning The People. It also appears in shortened form as *Nishnabe.*

Anishinabe-waki: Algonkian for Land of the People, or simply, Indian country.

Anthro: A slang abbreviation for anthropologist, commonly used by contemporary Indians.

Apple: A slang word denoting one of our own people who thinks or lives more like a white than an Indian; red on the outside but white on the inside.

Cabolclo: A Tupi-Guarani word meaning copper colored.

Hau: A Sioux word meaning either hello or yes.

Hau Kola: Sioux words meaning "Hello, friend."

Hi-yo-po: Sioux for "Let's go!"

Lakota: The name of the western, or Teton division of the Sioux nation.

Maka Meen-de-ga: Shawnee for Black Owl.

Paha Sapa: The Sioux name for the sacred Black Hills of South Dakota.

Pejuta-Sapa: A Sioux phrase meaning coffee.

Wakan Tanka: The Sioux word for God.

Wasicun: The Sioux word for white man.

Wi: The Sioux word for sun.

The buffalo grass is still.
Dust devils die from neglect.
     I know how they feel.
I am Indian.

Like unborn dust devils
     I wait for a fresh breeze.
It comes. Dust devils are born.
     I listen. I learn. I grow strong.
I am Indian.

A body of many parts
     Scattered to the four winds.
My mouth speaks in many tongues.
     Like dust devils, all are the whole.
I am Anishinabe!

1
WHAT
INDIANS?

We did not ask you white men to come here. The Great Spirit gave us this country as a home. You had yours. We did not interfere with you. . . . We do not want your civilization! We would live as our fathers did, and their fathers before them.

—CRAZY HORSE, OGLALA LAKOTA

New Mexico . . . July 9, 1976—12:35 P.M.

The desert heat played its wavering magic in the noonday sun, turning the hard line of tanks into a shimmer of translucent gray-green ghosts. They seemed out of place in the gold and red desert, as if they had been dropped by some cosmic accident into the middle of a Dali landscape. The men had long since been driven from the furnacelike interiors of their tanks, and were huddled in small clumps, sweat-drenched figures seeking what little shade the boxlike forms afforded.

The full armored battalion stretched in a ragged line for over two miles. It was flanked on each side by infantry and light artillery units which had been hastily thrown together from California and Texas National Guard posts. Two full divisions of fighting men and their equipment ringed the "hot spot" and sat waiting, baking in the desert noon. The men were not happy.

Three thousand yards in front of the line of tanks,

a lone figure sat astride a paint pony, watching. He was stripped to the waist. A .30 caliber carbine rested easily across the shoulder of his mount. His long black hair stirred in the light, hot breeze, beneath the strip of red cloth that circled his head and tied in a knot above his right ear. His impassive expression was broken only by a broad slash of black paint which arched across his dark, high cheekbones and aquiline nose. This was the enemy.

At least he was as much of the enemy the soldiers had seen in five days. The particular man and horse had changed at regular intervals, but there was always one man and one horse standing motionless every three miles, across the desert. From a distance of three thousand yards, they all looked alike to the troops.

Five days. Just five days ago the feathers had hit the fan. On July 4, 1976, right in the middle of the two hundredth birthday of the United States of America, the Navajo, Sioux, Mohawk, Apache, and Pueblo nations had declared their independence.

Preston, Oklahoma . . . June 27, 1976—8:15 A.M.

The morning sun caught the dust devils as they chased each other across the path of Howard McAfee's late-model Ford. The early Oklahoma summer had brought with it the usual hot dry spell. A smile crossed McAfee's sunburned face as he turned into the small parking lot next to his office building. He felt relaxed after his three-day fishing holiday.

The empty lot gave him a curious twinge but he pushed it aside. He unlocked the door and was about to enter when the rumble of heavy trucks drew his attention toward the highway. A convoy of National Guard trucks and equipment was passing the Bureau of Indian Affairs district office, on its way west and out of town. Howard paused halfway through the door to watch. He waved at the first truck. He knew the driver but got no response.

"Strange," he said out loud. Howard often talked to himself. He blamed it on living around people who wouldn't talk to him. "My Indians," Howard called them. "Very strange. That's the second National Guard unit to leave on maneuvers this week. Some of my Indians, too, I imagine. Oh, well . . . . "

As he let the door shut behind him, the phone started ringing. "To work," he thought, and crossed the empty outer office into his own.

"Good morning. Bureau of Indian Affairs. May I help you?"

"This is Azile Whitefish. Let me speak to your area director." *The* man in Washington, Azile Whitefish, director of the Bureau of Indian Affairs and a full-blood Osage from northern Oklahoma. He made McAfee nervous.

"Yes, sir! This is Howard McAfee, Mr. Whitefish. What can I do for you?" McAfee sat down, at attention.

"Where is everybody down there? I've been calling you for half an hour. You fire all your help?" Whitefish sounded strained.

"No, sir. Actually, I can't say." McAfee's mind raced. Where the hell *was* everybody? "Just got in . . . long weekend, ya know. My people haven't come in yet. How can I help you?"

"Help me? Sounds like you'd better help yourself. As a matter of fact, that's why I called." The voice stopped, then began again. "McAfee, have you noticed anything strange around your area . . . er, with the Indian population, I mean?"

"Well . . . " Howard's mind flashed to the two Indian National Guard units, his empty office. He shoved them from his thoughts. "Well . . . no, Mr. Whitefish. I know my people pretty well. Nothing strange down here."

There was a muffled cough on the Washington end. "O.K., McAfee, since you *know* your people so damn well, I suggest you find out where your office staff is. All Indians, aren't they? You call me if you hear anything, even if you don't understand it!"

The line went dead. McAfee couldn't have replied anyway—his mouth hung wide open.

Howard could have closed his mouth and relaxed. He was the area director of an office of the Bureau of Indian Affairs, and, as he would soon learn, his district no longer had any Indians in it. One might say that Howard McAfee had just become unemployed.

*Consulate of the Republic of India—New York City
...July 2, 1976—2:33 P.M.*

"Wait! Quiet everybody!"

All conversation ceased and seven men turned their attention toward the television.

" ... Troops now massed along the West German border are said to be the largest single deployment of Communist Bloc forces since the Hungarian Revolt in 1956 .... "

"This looks like it!" A voice broke the silence. Glances were exchanged. "Let's wait a few minutes to be sure. If the president acts now, so can we." The voice was calm and even, but a note of excitement rang in its delivery.

" ... latest from the Pentagon .... It has been twenty-four hours since the president ordered the Ready Strike Force mobilized. Reports now indicate that by midnight another forty-five thousand American troops and all necessary equipment will have assumed positions opposing the Russian forces. General Tucker Sherman reported ... "

"That's it!" The man stood up, reached for his suit coat, straightened his tie, and adjusted the otter skin wrappings that covered his braids. Roy Bear Walks Backward started for the door.

"Mr. Nadcarny, please ask your ambassador to file our declaration of war with the secretary general at the United Nations." Roy took the warm handshake of the Indian diplomat. "The people of Anishinabe-waki are grateful to you and the republic of India, sir. Now we can straighten out just who the real Indians are, eh? Gentlemen, *Hi-yo-po!*"

South Dakota . . . July 3, 1976—Evening

The subtle changes taking place on the several Sioux reservations had gone unnoticed all summer. Off-reservation families always returned to take part in the various tribal powwows held at that time of year, and the whites living in the small towns and on the reservations hadn't noticed that this year there seemed to be more Indians around than usual. It was always so hard to figure Indians anyway. Why they left this place only to return year after year was a mystery to most white folk.

At first, the barring of whites in the late sixties and early seventies from most of the "profitable" ceremonies had caused anger. The long-term, superficial result was that the annual increase in the area's Indian population had been ignored once it had ceased to mean more money. Person to person, face to face, it was something else. After the Wounded Knee affair in 1973, the longstanding undercurrent of racism began rising to the surface. Indians were now openly discouraged from patronizing more and more public places. Their earning power had been reduced by their own desire to retain or restore the dignity of what was left of their culture and religion. They were no longer willing to sell their trinkets or their ceremonies for the amusement of the tourists, a change which melted the plastic smiles hung each year on the greedy faces of white promoters. If these Indians were not going to add to the local coffers, they sure as hell weren't going to benefit from the improvements of white "civilization," most of which had been financed by using the Indians as a tourist attraction.

For the Lakota, the most important of ceremonies was the Sun Dance. This ritual was the focus of their religious belief, the highest expression of personal commitment to the people and to the Great Mystery. Once suppressed by white lawmakers and driven underground, the Sun Dance had again taken its place in the lives of most Lakota. The ritual piercing of the flesh was not the brutal torture most outsiders believed it to be, but an expression of the deepest spiritual and personal sacrifice of the physical and mental being to the service of one's people that one individual could offer. The white man had been barred because he wished to make a circus of it.

The return had begun as usual in late spring. Families arrived to be reunited and enjoy the closeness of the old Indian lifestyle. They came in pickups and beaten-up old cars, so overloaded with people that their springs groaned for relief. Some came in new cars paid for by hard work in the reeking cities of the white man. Others, mostly kids, hitchhiked. They had traveled from towns close by and from city ghettos or suburbs as far away as New York and California. What the white man hadn't noticed was that this year they didn't leave. They simply had come home—for good. The land of the fabled Sioux was once more peopled by the fabled Sioux. Some of the more astute local whites were disturbed to find, as they said, "an Injun behind every rock."

The weeks preceding the grand celebration of the Fourth of July had hosted, away from non-Indian eyes, a series of meetings. They were long and serious, accented by visits of faces new to Sioux country. Navajo, Hopi, Mohawk, and Apache dotted the meetings of the new and nonelected tribal leaders. The so-called tribal council, duly elected in duly manipulated BIA elections, did not attend. They were off, as usual, either wheeling and dealing with white ranchers for Indian land-leases, or ensuring their reelection by hobnobbing with their local BIA area director. In this case, the director was an Ivy League Cherokee, unrecognizable as an Indian to anyone except, perhaps, his mother. This meant nothing to the Sioux, since they didn't know his mother.

Though serious, the mood of these new leaders was one of joyful expectation. Their planning sessions were well attended by ex-servicemen who had learned the secrets of war—not in the old way, from a blood uncle, but from a different Uncle in the steaming jungles and rice paddies of Southeast Asia. Experts in everything from small arms modifications to counterinsurgency gathered to share their knowledge. It was against this background that the new generation of war chiefs had emerged. New names like Turning Hawk, Tall Warrior, Standing Elk were on the lips of the people. These were the men who had stepped forward to direct and plan.

The customary ceremonies and powwows were held on schedule, or as close to it as Indian Time allowed. But at the same time, the dusty roads in the back country were alive with unusually heavy traffic as families rushed to relocate in areas away from the reservation boundaries. There was a nonstop flow of pickups, stake trucks, horse trailers, and anything else that could be loaded with food, clothing, and the odd assortment of weapons which had found its way from gun dealers in Kansas City, Denver, and Chicago into the hands of the Lakota.

Units made up of former paratroopers and special forces veterans (the army brass always felt that Indians made good behind-the-line fighters), had scoured the lands west of the Missouri River, picking out locations for defense lines to be set up. By the evening of July third, everything but the physical occupation of these positions had been accomplished.

On that evening, a special lodge had been erected near the sacred Black Hills—*Paha Sapa*—and within a stone's throw of Mount Rushmore. Isolated from all but nature's own monuments, the structure's painted skins hung on pine poles took on a beautiful and holy aspect. A sweat lodge, located nearby on the bank of a small stream, added to the scene that would have driven an ardent anthro right up the stone face of old Thomas Jefferson, who watched blindly a few miles away.

The lodge awaited the war chiefs. They were now the leaders of the Lakota—the first real chiefs in a hundred years. Each had come alone, purified himself in the sweat lodge, and prayed before joining the rest inside the lodge. One old man had been assisted in this effort by two girls. After seating him at the place of honor opposite the door of the lodge, and placing a blanket around his shoulders, his two great-grand-daughters left quietly, without a word, to wait at a respectable distance outside until he needed them.

With the movements of modern guerrilla warfare already set in motion across South Dakota, the war chiefs of the Sioux prepared to reenact—for real—the custom of warrior talk. Each in his own turn stood and spoke to his brothers of deeds to be performed, sacrifices to be made. They did not use English here. They spoke the tongue of their fathers with renewed heart. Each in his turn spoke of things white men would fear to say to his fellows. They spoke long and well.

The old man had said nothing. He sat while those younger spoke of war, of glory, of the wrongs done to the Sioux and their new allies. He listened. At times, his eyes closed. His hands were so still it appeared that he had passed from the living. A pipe of the sacred red stone was cradled in his palms. The pipe had seen other hands—the hands of his father and his father's father. The bowl was shiny and dark from the oil rubbed in by the gentle fingers of three generations of Lakota.

"*Grandfather.*" A young man, whose long hair was wrapped in the fur of the otter, spoke. He waited for the old man to open his eyes.

"*Grandfather,*" he began again, "*we have spoken what is in our hearts. We are all brothers and allies. We wish to hear your words.*"

The old man looked around the circle. He did not rise. The days had passed when he could move without the aid of his great-granddaughters. But now, like storm clouds building over *Paha Sapa*, he began visibly to gain strength.

"*Lakota . . . you know me. When my eyes first opened and the Great Mystery put life into my body, the Lakota were still warriors. My father was a man of many great deeds. He fought the Wasicun at the Greasy Grass, the place they now call the Little Big Horn. He fought with honor.*" The old man paused.

"*My father's father rode many war trails against those who were our enemies—the Pawnee, the Crow—and died with great heart at the Battle of a Hundred Slain when the blue-coats first tried to steal our land. You know this to be so.*" He waited for the negative reply he knew would never come.

"*It has been many winters since the Lakota sat in war*

council. The winters have been long and cold. Often our women and children have gone without meat and warm clothing. Lakota! Is this not so?"

The threadbare blanket slipped from his shoulders and revealed his grandfather's war shirt. The hand-stitched beading and porcupine quillwork caught the light of the small fire. The firelight erased the age from the ancient face as it recalled other such councils, long since silent, beneath the dark skies that had known Crazy Horse, Gall, Hump. His slight body took on the agelessness now building within the masterful oratory of his ever-quickening mind. His back straightened; he held the pipe firmly in his left hand while his right accentuated his speech with the sweep and grace of an eagle in flight.

"Lakota! My uncle taught me to walk like a man, even when the black-robes tried to make us drop our heads like beaten dogs. The sun has been dark these many winters, but now it brings back life to the Sacred Hoop of the People. The breasts of our young men again show the scars given to the People as a sign of renewed life. Is it not so?"

"Hau! Hau!" The affirmative words came as though one heart had united the circle of seated men.

"I do not know what the Wasicun now thinks. I do not know his weapons. My knowledge of these things is of another time. It is not for me to decide which path is best for our nation." He looked into the unwavering gaze of his great-grandson; pride and sadness filled his eyes. *"Our young men have fought the Wasicun's battles. They have fought in many far-off places strange to our people. Many*

have not come home again. They have used his weapons and learned of the evil and death his war can bring to the land of the Lakota. But my friends, has he not brought evil and death here without war? Has he not killed the spirit of our young with his empty words and promises? Has not he made their hands grow greedy and their hearts wither? Has he not turned many of them from the way given us by Wakan Tonka?

"Lakota! What then will we lose if we fight? Our lives? What are lives to those who walk with no spirit in the body? What are lives if our bellies are empty and our babies crippled before they take their first step?

"It is not for me to decide, my friends. Very soon, my spirit will journey to the Outer World and these useless limbs will become grass. It is not for me to tell you young men to fight. But now the path is chosen! The sound of drums fill Paha Sapa once more. If this path is chosen, then I say: Lakota! Brave up! It is a good day to die!"

Like an ember that had burst into flame only to lose its life in that brief flare, the light of youth faded from the old man as quickly as it had come. John Captures Many Horses had given his last speech. It would be long remembered, for those around the circle knew they had heard a warrior speak the words of many strong hearts long since quiet in the land of the Lakota.

Joel Turning Hawk waited until the blanket had once again been placed around the old man's shoulders. His boots and faded denim trousers marked a strange contrast to the fur-wrapped braids that framed his dark features. His bare chest showed the scars of the Sun Dance, the very scars his great-grandfather had just spoken of. The warrior rose. He could hear his own heart pounding and could feel the proud blood it pumped in his breast. Thoughts flashed through his head with lightning speed. He knew what he said would be listened to by the men who gathered here. As proud as he felt, he also felt the weight of responsibility. He knew his words might die along with his nation if it chose the wrong path. But he also knew that at that moment he was a leader among leaders.

As a boy he had been disappointed when a cousin had been given a chance at a white man's education. He now saw clearly why he had not been given that chance. His place was here. It was now, and always, where he belonged. He knew that without question as he began to speak.

"My Brothers. My great-grandfather's words will not fall away. They are not to be blown to the horizon like so much dust. His words are those of many who have gone before us. We, here now, do know the Wasicun as he has said. I have fought for him as have many of you.

"This land given to our people by the Great Mystery has felt the scorching sweep of the Wasicun's ironclad fist. His evil and death has touched even the most distant part of this world. He is strong and he is many. Perhaps even the Lakota, the Navajo, and the Mohawk together cannot conquer him. Then let it be so. But first let us show the Wasicun that his evil and empty promises have not begotten him an easy vic-

tory. Let him know that we are men and will honor the greatness of those whose memory he has tried to erase!"

Joel bent down and gently took up the medicine bag which lay beside his rifle. Placing it to his chest, he stroked the soft brown fur with a reverence few men now understand. Raising his eyes, he could see the stars plainly through the open smoke flaps.

"Until we win, or until we die, we will fight. This time we will not accept the Wasicun's living death. Either we will walk like men or we will walk with those who died like men. These are my words."

Joel Turning Hawk, a twenty-seven-year-old Rosebud Sioux, had spoken. There was no more to be said. At sunrise, the new nation would be at war with the United States. The outcome might not be good, but, for these people, it could hardly get worse.

New Mexico . . . July 4, 1976—0600 hours

Pfc. Charlie Graham ambled across the compound past the showers and latrine. His starched fatigues were rumpled although he'd put them on fresh five minutes before. Everything Charlie wore looked rumpled. Actually, it was Charlie himself who looked rumpled. It was probably his long frame—Charlie was six feet, five inches and very self-conscious about it. He stooped a lot which made him appear very old and worn. Poor Charlie was nineteen but looked sixty-five. He was the kind of guy who always stepped in front of the one snowball in ten that had a rock in it.

Being a magnet for mishap and misfortune had given Charlie a sixth sense that picked up trouble before it happened. It never helped because he still always walked straight into it, but at least he was prepared for the worst.

That morning, Charlie was mentally preparing himself. It was going to be one of those days and Charlie could smell it.

The fresh-looking captain Charlie passed on his way to the mess had no such second sight. Capt. Harvey Michaels was enjoying the nice morning. His only regret was that he was stuck in camp on a holiday. But work at the new dam site was behind and had to be caught up. He took a deep breath and started for the officers' mess. It was then that he looked up and saw them.

Approaching out of the morning sun was a large group of horsemen. Harvey had seen many riders since he'd been stationed in the Southwest, but never so many at one time, and never on the site. Their ponies hardly made a dust, so they appeared to be in no hurry. It was not until they crossed the first line of tents that Harvey could see the weapons. "Probably hunters," he thought to himself. He'd often seen hunters in the area. But then he saw their painted faces.

"What the hell?" Harvey was transfixed by a sight he'd only seen in movies. His attention was diverted by the crunch of gravel as Lt. Tom Baker approached.

"By God, will you look at that! Ever see anything like it?"

"No, sir . . . can't say I have, sir." Baker looked over his shoulder. "But if you turn around you can see it again."

"Huh?"

"They're coming in from all directions, sir."

Maj. Paul Nelson, commanding officer of the Army Corps of Engineers unit, joined the two men. No one spoke. They were all too busy watching, turning in one direction and then the other as the horsemen moved slowly between the rows of tents until the area was well covered. Three lead horsemen approached the group of officers and halted ten feet away, rifles braced on their knees. Each wore a strip of red cloth around his head and a black band of paint across his face.

"Is one of you the officer in charge of this unit?" The lead horseman spoke in a slow, measured way. Eyes hard, features unmoving, he waited for an answer that seemed to take forever.

The major finally regained control and stepped forward.

"I'm Major Nelson. What can I do for you?"

"Surrender."

The major grinned. "Movies, huh?"

"No movie."

"Uh . . . you did say surrender?"

"Yes."

"Why?"

Calmly and slowly, the man leveled his rifle with one hand, pointing it dead at the major's chest. "Because you haven't got any other choice."

Nelson looked around uneasily, then his eyes riveted back to the rifle. "Now look, Chief, this is not what I call funny."

"Nor I, Major . . . . And I am not a chief."

"O.K., Sitting Bull! Now get your goddamn people out of here! The fun is over!"

"My name is Edward Wolf Stands In Water, and

this is not being done to amuse you." With a quick movement he snapped a round into the chamber of his rifle. "I repeat, Major: Surrender."

Charlie had been right. It was not going to be a nice day. Not for the Army Corps of Engineers, anyway.

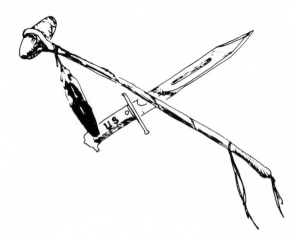

*St. Regis, on the New York–Quebec border
. . . July 4, 1976—Midmorning*

While luckless Charlie and his fellow enlisted men
were being transferred to the edge of the new state of
Cabolclo, and the unit's officers processed into a POW
holding area, a Royal Canadian Mounted Police patrol
car sat facing a barricade thrown up across the main
highway at the Canadian side of the Mohawk reserve.
The sun was climbing toward noon and orders from
headquarters had just been received.

Before sunrise, the entire reserve had been closed
off by the Mohawk people. The line the whites had
drawn on paper to separate their own nations had
been erased, and the Mohawk were all one people
again. Not that they had ever considered themselves
otherwise. The white officials of Canada and the
United States who lived within the boundaries of
the former reservation were the first to learn of this.
Communication lines had been severed and only
one message had been sent to the outside. It was

directed to Washington, D.C. and it read: "BIA is POW." No explanation. They would understand later.

The two hapless mounties were about to make the same mistake the "Light Brigade" had. Their's was not to reason why. Headquarters had assumed the roadblock was just another protest. Their orders had simply been to ram the damn thing and then proceed onward to find out who had dared put it up. The RCMP patrol car pulled out. No Indians were in sight.

Seconds later a bullet made its cobweb pattern on the windshield, but still the mounties were undeterred. They simply told the dispatcher they were being fired upon and were proceeding according to orders. It turned out to be a bad decision. Indians and mounties have a long history of bad feeling. Sadly, for these two officers, the Indians were about to start repaying old debts, with interest.

The car cleared the debris of the barricade at sixty miles per hour and immediately found itself under deadly accurate sniper fire. Both front tires were blown out even before the first crack of a rifle was heard. The driver braked and pulled the car out of its skid. The officers flung themselves behind the cover of their open doors and drew their revolvers. They desperately tried to locate the source of the shots. Failing that, they picked out a likely clump of trees and snapped off several rounds. There was a short pause and then, without further warning, both officers were down and wounded.

Having drawn blood and clearly made their point, the invisible snipers allowed the officers to make their retreat on foot to the barricade line. Once they were clear of the car, a well-placed tracer round set off the fuel tank. Reinforcements halted short of the reserve boundary and assisted the two men who were frantically trying to outrun what they were sure would be more accurate fire. But the Mohawks seemed to be content to wait, for the time being at least, for reaction from the increasing number of mountie units pulling into position on and off the highway.

What had begun as a quiet coup now screamed the ungodly curse of human warfare. Once unleashed, there was no recall. The course had to be run; the price paid; the lives spent. An hour later, a Mohawk warrior was to die from police bullets on the American side of the border. It had begun in earnest, and death began collecting its bills. The question of Crazy Horse would be asked again: "What price our land?" As before, there would be no sane answer.

Capitol Building—Washington, D.C.
. . . July 4, 1976—1:15 P.M.

The president paused, frowning disapproval as he glanced quickly over his left shoulder. He caught the eye of an aide, glowered meaningfully and, without further delay, continued his speech, satisfied that the muttering just off the rostrum would be silenced.

" . . . and now," he resumed with complete composure, "on this day, two hundred years after the birth of our great nation, we have come here to rejoice together. In no other land, at no other time in the memory of man, has a nation . . . a unified people . . . accomplished what this nation, these people have." Applause swept the crowd.

"Now, once again, this great nation is face to face with another test, equal to that at the time of its birth. Aggression raises its ugly head in Europe, and we must not fail . . . we cannot fail . . . . In 1976 as in 1776, we will go forward . . . . "

The muttering had not abated. The president could hear voices above the crowd's clatter. His aide stood slightly to one side of the group he had been sent to admonish. His face was chalk white, his arms hung limp at his sides. With mouth agape, he slowly shook his head, unwilling to believe what he had just heard. His lips formed words without sound. He was pushed aside by a young army officer, but continued his mute performance unnoticed.

General of the Army W. Tucker Sherman scanned the third message scribbled in the longhand of his aide-de-camp, who had been rushing back and forth from a recently arrived communications vehicle.

"Damn . . . oh, damn it to hell! Not now, not to-day! It's impossible . . . . It's . . . goddamn . . . it's un-American . . . ." He was talking to himself.

Vice-Admiral Wallace H. Harden said nothing, as was his custom. Instead, he removed his cap and flicked a bead of perspiration from his forehead with little regard for where it landed. It landed on the vice-president of the United States. His head lowered, his hands plunged deep in his trouser pockets, Vice-President Thad Browning looked for all the world like a lost little boy, despite his graying hair.

"We'd better tell him now." He spoke to no one in particular. "Someone had better tell him now." Suddenly life sprang back into his body. "I said *now*, god-damnit! Before he finishes that stupid speech." The vice-president had read the speech.

The crowd, fanned out in every possible direction from the Capitol steps, began to notice the disquieting murmur and activity on the raised presidential podium. Secret Service men instinctively edged closer to the president, who now joined in the uneasy silence of the crowd. He stepped back from the microphone and angrily turned to the Speaker of the House. The Speaker rose to answer what he knew was not going to be a friendly request. The president was not at all nice when he got angry, and his clenched fist and pinched lips were definite signs that he was very angry.

"Josh, get over there and find out what that gaggle of geese are doing!" The Speaker crossed quickly to the vice-president, who was just stepping onto the platform, his face drawn with anticipation. It was up to him to give the president the unpleasant news. It was hardly a pleasure watching the chief executive blow his top in public view, and there was very little doubt that was exactly what was going to happen.

"Thad." The Speaker could sense the coming explosion too. "What the hell's going on?" Without answering, the vice-president brushed past him. "Well for Christ's sake!" he burst out, catching his balance.

Secret Service men moved in en masse, nearly circling the two top men of the government. Like buffalo cows protecting their young, they faced outward, waiting for the approaching danger. The marine detachment had quietly gone to fixed bayonets at the guard position on order from the chief of the Secret Service, who stood at an observation post speaking in a low but frantic voice into his walkie-talkie. He could feel the tension growing in the massive crowd spread out in front of him. "What? No, I don't know," he sputtered into the plastic box. "Just get me every man you can find over here, and do it now!"

Summoning up the remnants of his composure, the vice-president cleared his throat. "Mr. President." He cleared his throat again. "Mr. President, our troops have been fired on."

The president didn't move. He didn't even blink. "Fired on?" His face was livid and panic flashed behind his glazed eyes. "West Germany . . . it's happened . . . World War III . . . ."

"No, sir." The vice-president felt his composure slipping as the panic in the president's eyes came and went like the shutter on a camera. "In New Mexico, sir . . . ."

"Russians in New Mexico?" Panic mushroomed into full horror.

"No, Mr. President . . . er . . . Indians . . . ." Browning groped for words. " . . . Army Corps of Engineers . . . ."

"Indians! What the hell are you talking about? Indians! What Indians? You mean *Indian* Indians? Like Tonto? *Our* Indians? Oh no, not again!" The president paled.

"Goddamnit, Thad! You mean you stopped my speech for that? It wasn't three years ago that we went through this with that bunch in South Dakota! Are you going to tell me this is so damn important it couldn't wait an hour?"

"Mr. President, it's not . . . well, it's not quite the same."

"What do you mean, not the same? What the hell they got this time? An army?"

"Yes, sir, in a way . . . I think they do . . . . " The vice-president heard his voice quiver. "The combined forces of the newly formed Anishinabe-waki Democracy have sent a message to the office of the secretary general of the United Nations," he was reading from a scrap of yellow paper, "declaring their independence and informing the ambassador to the UN, the honorable representative of the United States, that a state of war now exists between the aforesaid government and the United States." He continued to stare at the paper as if expecting to see more writing appear at any moment, and to wait for the ensuing explosion, neither of which was about to happen. Only a barely audible "Shit!" could be heard from the direction of the chief executive.

The president sat down in a nearby chair which immediately collapsed under his weight.

The White House—Washington, D.C. . . .
July 4, 1976—6:10 P.M.

The office of the president, in the East Wing of the White House, was very quiet. The president sat behind the large desk, flexing his numb fingers against the bandage on his left wrist. He had sprained the wrist when his highly placed body had landed on the lowly floor of the presidential podium.

The president had just returned from the White House War Room. It was no joke, at least not for the Army Corps of Engineers. Fifteen officers were now officially listed as POWs in New Mexico alone. No dead, but there were thirty-eight reported wounded. The injuries had been caused mostly by broom handles wielded by women at the site of a new dam on the already overdammed Rio Grande. The men had simply stood back, their arms trained on the new POWs. It had not been an orderly withdrawal, hardly worthy of study at the "Point."

The president looked up at the large map sent over from the Department of the Interior. Red areas in-

dicated reservations within the boundaries of the new
Anishinabe-waki nation. At the bottom, a color-coded
legend in hand-printed letters read "war zones"—red
for known Indian-controlled land; yellow for those as
yet uncertain. The president not only saw red, but he
absent-mindedly thought how well the color fit the
situation.

He didn't really mind the idea of a small war. As a
matter of fact, he had told the CIA to find one the
country could get into. But not at home, for God's
sake. And not now! It was the timing that galled him.
He had spent six years planning this bicentennial. Six
goddamn years of planning, planning, planning—not
to mention the number of payoffs he had had to make
to get everyone in line.

His blue eyes glinted like steel beneath heavy
brows. The widow's peak at the top of his high, fur-
rowed forehead gave him a disconcertingly evil appearance. Swinging his gaze to a tall young man who
stood at his right, the president's eyes grew even
harder. Dark, almost oriental eyes set in a handsome
copper face returned the president's glare with equal
feeling, though none of it showed on the even features.
The two men plainly had a mutual dislike for each
other.

"Well, Congressman Small Wolf?"

"Yes, Mr. President?" the man replied.

"Well, you're my expert on Indian affairs. You're
our up-and-coming young Indian congressman, and
you're always whining about my Indian programs. If

you're so goddamn smart, what the hell started all this?" By the time he finished, his voice had hit a strident peak. Aides, advisors, and even the vice-president flinched. The congressman didn't. Grinning slightly, he spoke in a quiet voice.

"Well, Mr. President, off hand I'd say it was a man named Christopher Columbus."

Everyone in the room stood gaping, except the vice-president, who had closed his eyes. The president slammed his fist down hard.

"What the hell kind of answer is that?" He was really shouting now. "I want to know why you weren't aware of this! I want to know who is behind it! I want to know why in the name of Satan you aren't in jail!"

Despite the tension in the air, the young congressman began speaking softly, as if he intended to unnerve the president even more.

"Mr. President," he said, taking a step forward. "Number one, I truly believe this started with that lost Italian bastard on that goddamn Spanish ship. I also informed you, upon taking this post, that unless your policies changed, the Indian people were bound to do something. But I honestly didn't think it would go this far, not even after Wounded Knee."

He slowly crossed the room. The attention of the men around him was intense.

"Next, sir, just because I'm an Indian doesn't give me an inside line to every house, hogan, wickiup, or long-house meeting on this continent. Indians don't work like you people. They trust each other but keep things close to their chest. Because I'm here with you, even my own tribe has grave doubts about my honesty. Frankly, I often wonder about it myself." The young Indian paused, looked at the floor. Raising his eyes, he looked directly at the president.

"Mr. President." The words were slow and deliberate. "If I knew who, why, when, or anything else about this, I can't honestly say I'd tell you. As for why I'm not in jail, I've broken no law."

With that he excused himself, saying, "With all due respect, sir. I'll be leaving Washington for home," he jerked a thumb at the map, "for the war zone, tonight. I trust you'll have enough guts to face a few facts for once. The next time we meet, I hope you'll know me better. At least, maybe you'll respect my people as people. Gentlemen." He left the room.

The silence was broken by General Sherman. "Mr. President, sir? Should we have him detained?"

"General, I don't give a damn what you do with that bastard. No wait, put him under house arrest, for now."

The president crossed the room. Hands folded behind him, he gazed out the window. For the first time, the day's events had begun to sink in. His mind had begun sorting all that had taken place; almost without conscious effort, each piece of information was separated and organized. Moments passed. The men in the room had begun a low discussion among themselves. The president was set apart from them by what he was, the chief executive. As one of his predecessors had put it, he was where "the buck stops."

He knew the situation in Europe was already precarious, and now the day's events had added new fuel to the smoldering fire. It was impossible to assess just how this would effect the U.S. position abroad. He had little doubt the added strain would not help, but to what extent it would hurt, the president wished he could predict. Which countries would continue to support the U.S. as it faced enemies on two fronts, and which would not? He feared many of the allies might not be willing to turn their backs on America's Red Indians, as they were called in Europe.

The support of the republic of India would be very influential with many of the unaligned nations, as would their own sense of identification with the underdog Anishinabe nation. An old United States domestic problem had suddenly turned into an international hot potato, and the president didn't like what he saw ahead.

Bethesda, Maryland . . . July 4, 1976—7:59 P.M.

Congressman Edward Small Wolf returned to his house in Bethesda to find his wife, Susan, talking or rather shouting to a man at the front door. Two other men stood close by in embarrassed silence. A government car sat in the driveway.

"There's my husband now, you tell him." Susan was flushed; her black eyes glowed. Slight in stature, she was looking up at the tall man who was trying valiantly to hold his ground.

"Damn you! Who the hell do you think you are? The BIA? Well, you can take the I.D. card and cram it in your ear!" She accented her last suggestion with a swing of her arm that knocked the hat off the man who made a futile effort to get out of her way.

Standing beside his car, Congressman Small Wolf was in no rush to interrupt his wife's outburst. He had often been on the receiving end of it himself and he enjoyed watching another victim. The pretty little Pine Ridge Sioux had all the spunk of her great-grandfather. "Oh yes," thought Ed, "warrior blood flows in her veins."

"Gentlemen," the congressman nodded. "Now, Susan, we must not injure these nice officers." Turning to the agent who was adjusting his recently retrieved hat, he queried, "I assume you *are* officers?"

The tall man did the I.D. bit again. "Congressman Small Wolf, I'm Agent John Dawson, FBI." Turning to his companions, "This is Agent Anderson and Agent Thomas. It's my duty to inform you that you are under house arrest by order of the president of the United States."

"Just what does that mean?" Ed Small Wolf was looking straight into the big man's eyes. He was well aware of the meaning and Agent Dawson knew it. Nonetheless, Dawson gave the *pro forma* explanation.

"It means, sir, that you are not to leave your residence until we receive further orders."

"May I ask under what charge this action has been taken?" Ed held his temper in check.

"Executive order, sir. That's sufficient." Agent Dawson glanced at Susan Small Wolf, waiting for another explosion. There was none.

"Am I allowed to use my telephone?" Ed's jaws tensed up. He could feel the blood rising in his face.

"Yes sir, but I may as well tell you, the line is tapped."

"Of course. Now are we going to stand out here all night, or are you coming in?" Ed motioned toward the door.

"We have men at the rear, sir. We'll stay out here. Thank you for your cooperation, Congressman, Mrs. Small Wolf." Dawson touched his hat and the three men started toward their car.

Ed watched them settle down. He stepped inside and slammed the door. Susan watched her husband stare at the door for a long moment.

"Ed." She tried to keep her voice from breaking. She had been angry, but now she was beginning to feel frightened. "Ed, what's this all about? Why are you under arrest?"

"I'm sorry, honey, but that's 'we,' as in both of us. Haven't you heard? We're at war with the United States. The Sioux nation took to the warpath again . . . after a hundred years! Damn, I should be home, not here, in this, this . . . . Oh, hell!" He slumped down in a chair. "Some Indian! Can't even leave my house while my people take on the strongest nation in the world!"

"But Ed," Susan was almost crying, "you had nothing to do with it! You had no way of knowing this was going to happen!"

"Susan, we're Indians! We're Sioux! That's all that jackass in the White House cares about!" He got up and crossed to the kitchen to fix himself a drink. "You know, Susan, jackass or not, he's right. I should have known. *I should have known! Christ!* I guess it's a long way from Washington to Pine Ridge. Congressman, my ass! I'm not even an Indian anymore, just a goddamn make-believe white man."

"Ed, what are you going to do?" Susan had collected herself. She realized what her husband was saying. Nothing worse could happen to an Indian than to be cut off from his people. It had happened, though. It was the first time either of them had realized it.

"Think, Susan, just think for now. The Sioux can handle this or they wouldn't have done it." He wondered if he was right.

The Pentagon—Washington, D.C. . . .
July 5, 1976—2:05 A.M.

"Well?" General Sherman looked up from the stack of reports on his desk. "How did this happen? How did those damn Indians do it? For God's sake! They've closed off entire sections of the country!" He waved at a map on the wall, a duplicate of the one in the president's office. Chewing on a stub of a spent cigar, he directed his questions to an assorted group of men called up from the Pentagon War Room. He zeroed in when no one answered.

"Jackson, you got any answers?"

Col. Harold Jackson's black face clearly showed the strain of the past eighteen hours. He shifted his notes. "Sir, reports from intelligence indicate this thing was planned by experts. It appears we trained most of the men who are running the military end ourselves." He paused to see if his report was being listened to. It was.

"There are three main areas now under control of the Indians, or enemy." He cleared his throat. "They include the area in and around the combined Navajo,

Hopi, Pueblo, and Apache reservations in New Mexico and Arizona, and the three main Sioux reservations in the Dakotas, Standing Rock, Pine Ridge, and the Rosebud. Most of that area has been cut off since the first breakout. We aren't sure now just how they accomplished it, but they did. The third is the main Mohawk reservation at St. Regis. As far as present information goes, that area was also secured quickly by the enemy." He reached for a glass of water.

"Damn," he thought, "my grandmother is half Indian." Enemy. The word gnawed at his gut.

"Well?" General Sherman was impatient. "What about the other reservations? What about numbers? How many goddamn Indians are there, anyway? How many are we fighting?"

Jackson broke in. "General, let me impress on you that except for the civil forces wounded at St. Regis, the Indians haven't actually shot to kill. As far as we know, anyway, they have only taken prisoners and . . ."

"How the hell do you think we run a war anyway, Jackson? These red bastards started this didn't they? *They* filed a formal declaration of war with the UN didn't they? What the hell are you doing? Trying to defend that bunch of red bastards?"

Jackson choked back the urge to make an undiplomatic reply. Instead, he went back to the folder of papers in his lap.

"Sorry, General." He continued, "The BIA, Bureau of Indian Affairs, indicates there were seven hundred fifty thousand Indians in 1970. That is estimated to be near one million at this time, no explanation for the sharp rise, except that more people have admitted to being Indian for the past three years. 1973, 1974, and 1975 show large increases in many areas. The BIA says the areas in question hold approximately one third, maybe more, of that number. For some reason, Oklahoma hasn't shown any sign of action yet, and that is where most nonreservation Indians are located. Local Guard forces have been alerted. Unfortunately, so many are Indians, their strength has been cut by almost half. The Indians simply didn't report in. The two Indian units they had on maneuvers have disappeared. Fort Sill is still trying to absorb the slack. It's pretty unstable at this time. Guard units from other states are now being sent in. If our regular troops weren't tied down in Germany we . . . . " His voice trailed off. He shook his head and went on.

"Records indicate some decrease in population on other reservations in recent months. We're not sure if they were moving into zones now held by the Indian forces. Best guess is that they were. Population in metropolitan areas shows some curious shifts too. Too early to tell what it means, but it's a safe bet they'll prove to be in one of those three areas."

"O.K." The general turned his attention to the next man.

"Excuse me, General," the colonel broke in again. "We have another problem."

"Which is?" The general lit the stub of his dollar

cigar again. He looked sideways at the black man. He didn't like Indians, but then he didn't like blacks either. The general was a bigot and it showed.

"General." Jackson set down his glass. "The laws that deal with Indians are a bag of snakes. Right now we have people trying to determine just where we stand legally."

The general choked on the puff of smoke halfway to his lungs. "Legally! You goddamn idiot!" He turned on the colonel. "We've got a civil war on our hands and you want to go to court!" He was up and pacing back and forth.

"General!" the colonel shouted. "Will you let me finish?"

His tone took the general by surprise. "O.K., Colonel, continue, but it had better be good."

"The problem, sir," there was an edge on Jackson's voice, "the problem is that although Indians are citizens of the United States, Indian tribal governments are considered to be sovereign. Or at least we think so. The Navajos have been trying to get recognition from the United Nations since 1967. Until we are sure and have sorted out the mess the BIA has created to sustain its operation, we can only take a holding action."

"Oh, my aching ass! You *people* are all alike!" The general said what he meant and every man in the room knew exactly what he was saying.

Jackson stood up. "Sir, whether you like it or not, ninety-five percent of the land now under Indian control belongs to them, and by God, they just may have some legal right to it!"

After an uncomfortable silence, Sherman sat down. "O.K., Colonel, we'll hold. Now you had better get your ass in gear and sort out those laws. Gentlemen, that is all."

New Mexico—Indian Perimeter . . .
July 5, 1976—7:35 A.M.

"Well, smartass, what now?" The kid whose intelligence was in question slowly stuck his head out just enough to see over the sand dune. His shaky composure broke completely as a bullet shot sand into his eyes. Laughter drifted over to the two guardsmen, who were young, scared, and confused. "Well, once again, I say what now, smartass?"

"Oh, screw you!" Pfc. Howard rubbed his eyes. "Goddamn Indians! I don't believe any of this! In a minute we're gonna wake up and this will be gone. Including you, you smart bastard!"

"Well, my fellow guardsman," his buddy smiled, half buried in sand, "Gene Autry never got stuck like this on the late movie."

"O.K., Jack, wait till I string this stupid rifle and I'll sing you a little song." His vision cleared a little. "Ya know, I don't believe this! I just don't believe this."

"I know, you said that before." Jack Thompson

screwed himself deeper into the sand. "Why don't you tell that Navajo out there? I think he believes it. He believes he's gonna shoot us. Personally, I believe what he believes because he's coming pretty close to making us both believers!"

Another shot split the air; then silence. The desert has plenty of time; men seldom have enough.

"Hey, snowboys!"

"That goddamn Navajo!" Jack wanted to take a shot. Instead, he tried to dig himself a deeper hole. Looking up, he shouted, "Screw you, Navajo!"

Three shots rang out in quick succession.

"I ain't no Navajo! I'm Ute, you white bastards!" The Indian temporarily forgot himself.

"What the hell's a Ute?" Thompson asked.

"I think it's a small guitar. What the hell do I know about Indians? A week ago I was having problems with a Polack! Why can't we fight Polacks? I ain't never had anything against Indians!"

The Indian taunted the guardsmen from his vantage point on higher ground.

"Hey, white eyes!" Joe Taylor, a Ute from Ouray Reservation, laughed easily. "Why don't you guys just surrender? Either you ain't got no bullets or you can't shoot! How 'bout it?"

"Whatcha think, Jack?" There was a pause.

"Well, Jack, whatcha think?"

Jack didn't think, he just threw his rifle over the dune. "Oh, fuck it. I quit!"

"O.K.," Howard said, "if that's how you feel." And

he threw his rifle over. "I never wanted to shoot no-body anyhow."

"Now, that's better." Joe spoke loud enough for the two youngsters to hear.

"Stand up, soldier boys, hands on your heads." Joe zeroed in between the two figures standing fifty yards off. "Now walk this way, easy."

The two guardsmen started toward the Indian. This was no joke to Joe. Had one of those white boys broken to run, he would have been ready to drop him. His twenty-five years had hardly created any love for white men. Maybe it was because his father—the father he had never seen—was white, that he hated them.

"O.K., snowboys." His blue eyes were calm. "Easy does it or you'll buy yourselves some land . . . Indian land, you bastards!"

Jack's knees wanted to buckle. "What now, Chief?" He didn't sound as brave as he had hoped he would.

"One more 'Chief' out of you and I'll break your fuckin' jaw." From the tone of his voice, the two week-end warriors knew this guy wasn't kidding. "For your information, I do what I am told. Turn you over to the Indian police. To make you feel better, they're real bastards." He chuckled.

"O.K., smartass, what now?"

"Oh, shut up!"

Taylor retrieved his pony and swung easily into the saddle. He brought up the rear as they headed, at a slow walk, toward the high security compound area of the Indian police.

As part of the overall plan, the four-hundred-man Indian Police Force had grown to one thousand eight hundred men. They now took care of internal security on the Indian-held land, handled prisoner processing and interrogation, and acted as a clearing house for new recruits, such as Joe Taylor, sifting into the reservation. As Joe had said, the IPF was hardly a group of powder puffs. They were mean and they were thorough, and in a short time they had become professionals, hardly what the outside world would have expected of "lazy reservation Indians."

Capt. Emil Tall Warrior, an Acoma Pueblo, was the commanding officer of the IPF in what was now the state of Cabolclo in the new Anishinabe-waki Democracy. They also controlled areas still occupied by non-Indians within the secured perimeter. Captain Tall Warrior, with the accord of the council, had seen to it that these areas were secured and the citizens were not harassed. They were, for the time being, under tight martial law. Eventually, they would have the choice to leave or to stay. The local law enforcement officers had been placed under arrest until they could be removed to the border. They bitched a lot but, finding themselves on the receiving end of their own dirty stick, decided to surrender without a fight. Though Captain Tall Warrior had not allowed any unnecessary harassment of the officers, a few old scores did get settled on the way to the lockup.

Similar situations were in effect in the other two new Indians states of Lakota and Akwesasne. The high degree of organization and effective control of the IPF in all three states would surely have surprised the watchdogs at the bureau.

Captain Tall Warrior had grabbed only two hours of sleep in the last forty-eight. He was tired as he settled behind the beaten-up desk in the small office at the former BIA center.

"Gus, we got any coffee ready?"

"On your desk, Captain." Gus Wachee walked in from the rear of the building, zipping up his trousers. His short, stocky body moved lightly and quietly. "You look like hell, Captain."

"Thanks, Gus." The captain took a big gulp of the steaming black liquid. "Man! You left them old moccasins in the pot again! This tastes just like your feet smell!"

"I thought it was kinda good. Besides, nobody else'll take time to do it. All our women are too busy with feedin'. I tried to get some sent over from the mess tent, but they said it would have to wait."

"Too damn hot for coffee anyway." All the same, Tall Warrior finished it off. "Any word from the council?"

"Not in the past three hours." Gus was trying some of his own coffee. "You're right, Emil, it ain't too good, is it?"

Joe Taylor appeared in the doorway. The dust on his face had little streaks of sweat running though it.

"Captain?"

"Yeah?" Emil looked up.

"I just turned over two prisoners to the IPF. They

asked me to stop here. Some important word from the Sioux just came in. Chairman wants to see you."

"Thanks, son." The captain headed for the main building in a BIA vehicle.

Joe Eddie Morris flashed his winning smile as the captain entered the relative cool of the former agency center building.

"Captain." Joe Eddie nodded and continued to smile. "Gonna be hotter than a Taos whore, eh?"

"Yeah . . . and it ain't gonna be cool again until September!" Captain Tall Warrior paused just inside the door to let his eyes adjust to the dark interior of the building. He motioned toward two men engrossed in deep conversation at the far end of the corridor. They had noticed his entrance but gave no indication and continued to talk softly in Navajo.

"Know what's up, Joe Eddie?"

"Nope! Been sitt'n here so damn long I don't know nuth'n. Sure hope somebody can relieve me soon. Man, I'm pooped! Bet ya when I stand up, my ass falls off on the floor!" Though dark circles sat heavy beneath his eyes, the young man's sense of humor had not suffered as much as his hind parts.

The IPF captain had to push the thought of rest from his own mind as he half-listened to Joe Eddie's continued description of what he expected to happen on and about his body within the next few minutes. The Apache kid had a vivid imagination.

"Boy!" the captain broke into the running mono-
logue. "We only been at this war a couple of days!
What you gonna do when they start shoot'n at ya?
Come unglued?"

"Well, Captain," said Joe Eddie, hardly missing a
beat, "I don't figure they're gonna have anything to
shoot at us. With all that money the pres spent on this
goddamn birthday party, I doubt there's anything left
to buy bullets with."

"You figure the U.S. Army is just gonna play dead
and let us have our country back and do nuth'n, huh?"
Tall Warrior eased himself down in one of the straight
chairs lining the wall.

"Don't really know 'bout that, but if they got the
same guys running the show that had it when I was
in, we got it in the bag! Even if them bastards had a
ring through their nose with a string tied to it, they
still couldn't find their face. Them dumb bastards!" A
hearty laugh burst from Joe Eddie. Catching himself,
he gave a sheepish glance toward the two men down
the hall. Seeing that they ignored his levity, the flash
of teeth once again covered his face.

Playing with the buckskin strap on his surplus AR–
15, Joe Eddie sailed into a lively and not very kind
assessment of army brass's failures on even the most
basic level. It was one of Joe Eddie's favorite subjects.

For a guy from the reservation, Joe Eddie sure
talked a hell of a lot. He smiled a hell of a lot too.
Listening to the boy, the captain was sure Joe had
never seen a Wayne-Ford western. If he had, he would

be more careful of that stoic Indian image. In five minutes, Joe Eddie could destroy all that mound of celluloid trash it had taken Hollywood forty years to stack up.

"Captain Tall Warrior . . . . " The soft voice came from the end of the corridor and stopped the young Apache in mid-sentence—the only way to stop him.

"Captain Tall Warrior, we've news from the Sioux to discuss with you." Art Navarro was moving forward at his never-changing slow walk. His grayish, shoulder-length hair was tied back with a red strip of cloth. He looked every day of his forty-eight years. Weather and concern had taken an active part in adding to the darkness and age of his features, which had the glow of well-rubbed wood. His ready smile gave him the appearance of an old and trusted friend, even to those he did not know. It had surprised no one when he was elected tribal chairman three years before. Art had not let the Navajo people down and he was even more determined not to fail his new country. He had fought the government of the United States across the table for many years, and by now the idea of a rifle in his hands was welcome. "I'm getting something *straight* between us, for once," he liked to remark. One might have added to that, "and for the first time."

Tall Warrior met the two men halfway down the corridor and followed them into a sparsely and haphazardly furnished office. It was the chairman's wartime office. It was not quite a White House War Room, but it functioned, despite the fact that it didn't even have a telephone.

"As you know, Captain, our forces here have managed to carry out all preliminary objectives." Art counted on his fingers. "Number one, all U.S. Forces within our boundaries are now prisoners. Number two, all whites except for some hard-core resisters are under martial law. They will be held as is until the danger of U.S. air power reprisal is determined. Number three, all electric generating stations—Four Corners and the rest—have been shut down. L.A., Phoenix, and Denver must be in one hell of a mess without that power. Water pumping stations to L.A. and Phoenix have been closed. For the time being, we've got them running in circles." The friendly face broke into a broad grin. "Not bad for a start. Now about your hassle up front, Emil.... Got a cigarette, Hank?"

Vice-Chairman Henry Trujillo dug a pack of bent Camels from his shirt pocket and tossed them across the desk.

"Sorry, they're a little worse for wear—I slept on 'em." Like the others, Henry had slept when and where he could. For him, the where had been the back of his '57 Chevy pickup.

"Thanks, Hank." The chairman carefully worked at making a full cigarette from the twisted mess he had taken from the pack.

"Now, Captain . . . either of you got a light? I smoke too much, like the white-eye, eh?" Tall Warrior lit the chairman's cigarette and decided to try his hand at reconstruction himself. He grabbed one from the pack on the desk.

"As I started to say," the chairman went on in a more serious vein, "I heard some of your boys up front didn't like the 'Indian warrior' act."

"Well, Chairman." Tall Warrior was trying to light his piece of a Camel. "Some of 'em felt like it was silly. Figure they're tired of that ol' crap. Anyway, I think it'll be O.K. after they understand why."

"Emil, those weekend soldiers are already bugged." It was Hank's turn with the mass of paper and tobacco. "They don't understand why they can't just charge in and clean us out if all we got is a bunch of kids on horseback playing Injun." He gave up on the Camel and threw the whole mess in a wastebasket.

"They haven't seen what's behind those Injuns. Within a week, they'll be so pissed off at their C.O.'s game play'n, it'll be hard keep'n them in the sun all day long. Thanks to the image that movies have set up in the minds of those guardsmen, Indians can't fight worth a damn. They see Indians out there that look just like the ones in the movies, so it follows that they should be able to get three with one shot, just like the Duke. What they don't know is that behind each of those young warriors is a four-man backup team—no feathers, just automatic weapons, and fully equipped and mobilized. They'll probably know that soon but they still see only the old stereotype. With the sun, the dust, and everything else, their morale is going to go all to hell and it won't take long."

"O.K., Emil, you explain it to 'em. Make sure they understand it's got its purpose." The chairman slowly snubbed out his Camel with a look of utter disgust.

"About this message . . . we expect this to be the last for a while. The army's just about jammed us out." He picked up the single piece of paper on his desk. "The Sioux have been sending through their stuff along with word from the Mohawks, all in Navajo. Just like the army in World War II, eh?" The familiar grin came and went. "Their head war chief, Joel Turning Hawk, has carried out all his placements and secured his boundaries. For a youngster, he hasn't wasted any effort. The council of the Lakota was in full accord with his planning. From what I've heard, so am I. Met him last spring. He's a real firebrand."

"What about the Executive Council, Art?" Tall Warrior gave up on his cigarette with a healthy last drag, then crushed it out in the ashtray.

"Well, Emil, seems it's all going all right. They haven't been heard from since sending that message to the UN. 'Course we ain't had any way to contact them."

The chairman looked around for the pack of Camels. "Hank, ask that guard out there to go get in some coffee and cigarettes. Now, Captain, while Hank's taking care of my vices, you got anything you'd like to throw in? We'll get back to the Executive Council in a minute."

Hank stuck his head into the hall. "Hey, Joe Eddie! Run over to the mess tent and get a pot of black coffee and a couple packs of Camels, O.K.? We'll look after the chairman while you're out."

The entire secret service detachment for the chairman got up, swung his rifle over his shoulder, and headed out the door. His ass didn't fall off.

The chairman of Cabolclo now sat completely unprotected as his one-man secret service went for coffee and cigarettes. The apparent lack of concern about his safety could never have been understood in Washington. Simply put, Art Navarro was not afraid of his countrymen, nor had he ever done anything to cause them to fear him. Anishinabe-waki didn't have an H-bomb, but it obviously possessed a very important weapon that the major powers had long since lost, if they ever had it at all. In their rush to out-civilize each other, the major countries had forgotten that basic trust and respect is the strongest bond between men. Political systems have suffered in more than one area because this simple aspect of human behavior has become all but extinct. The Nishnabe nurtured trust, and it lived in men like Tall Warrior, Navarro, Turning Hawk, and even in the younger men like Joe Eddie. This antiquated idea of love among men is a powerful weapon.

Hank pushed his straw hat on the back of his head as he sat down. His close-cropped black hair was wet with perspiration.

"Ya know, Art, we got to get someone to relieve that boy. He's really beat."

"Well, I need a guard like I need a dead mule hung around my neck."

The chairman looked over at the captain. "Emil, when you leave, have one of your IPF men come over and give the boy some time off. Council says I need a guard so we won't argue the small shit." Art never argued for the sake of hearing himself talk. "Now, did your people have anything they want us to look at?"

"Only that business about the warrior image. Otherwise, we've got things working well with the troop command. As the man said, 'so far so good.' "

"Fine, Emil. If anything at all comes up, you get to us. Now, the Sioux say that Canada, along with some countries south, is raising hell with Washington." The grin was back. "Seems they think this little idea of an old-fashion Indian uprising might just spread. They want the U.S. to put an end to it now. 'Course this was expected and can't blame 'em. They've all been shit'n on Indians so long they should expect trouble."

"The Sioux say the Executive Council followed up the declaration of war with the manifesto yesterday. It should have been noted in the UN Security Council by now." The chairman pulled some papers from the top drawer of his desk. He handed one to the captain. The rest he stuffed back in the drawer.

"Here, Emil, you post this copy where your boys can read it. A man has the right to know the whole story if you're asking him to die."

Lakota, near Paha Sapa . . . *July 5, 1976*
—*Sundown*

The laws of the white men no longer ruled in the land of the Sioux. The old way would now be followed. Lakota could now be buried as they wished.

The sound of wailing was carried by a hot southern wind; across the sacred *Paha Sapa*, a slow rhythm of drums caressed the raw edges of time-worn rock.

The spirit of John Captures Many Horses had passed to the Outer World. When his eyes had opened for the first time, the Lakota had been warriors. His eyes had closed for the last time and the Lakota were warriors once again. His great-grandson, Joel Turning Hawk, stood alone next to the scaffold where the body of the old man rested. His eyes raised to the evening home of *Wi* and his arms outstretched, Joel said farewell to his beloved grandfather, a true warrior of the Lakota. His name would be recalled many times and his words would not fall away.

Oval Office of the President—Washington, D.C.
...July 5, 1976—11:55 P.M.

The president's hand hurt. He had removed the ace bandage too soon and it throbbed like hell. His mood was black as he stalked the area behind his desk like a trapped cat. He asked for action; he got nothing. He asked for information; he got little. He asked for aspirin because he had one hell of a headache; he got that, and it didn't help.

The president swallowed the aspirin and dropped down in his chair. The impact drove a tremor through his body that made his head and his hand ache even more.

"General!"

General Tucker Sherman's wandering mind was shocked back to the present. "Yes, Mr. President?"

"General, here we sit. As a matter of fact, not only do we sit, our entire second line of defense is simply sitting. Orders were given; wheels rolled; men moved ... and now, we all sit."

Sen. Keller Dillman of Maine grinned. "Well, Mr.

President, at least we are all doing the same thing for once."

"Senator Dillman, drink your scotch and try to understand the military." General Sherman's voice was harsh. "You damn civilians are what slows us down!"

Dillman took a sip of his drink and gave Col. Hal Jackson a knowing look.

"General Sherman, had we 'damn civilians' been at Mai Lai, you sure as hell would have been slowed down. Now you want to do the same thing again. I tell you, sir, your damn trench graves in the boondocks won't work here! The one at Wounded Knee was sealed in 1890—pictures and all, just like the Nazis— but it still haunts the American people. You want more of that? Another overkill? General, sir, you'd better thank Almighty God that someone slows you down once in a while."

The president's spine stiffened at the mention of the word overkill. Since that Asian mess six years before, he'd gotten no end of guff from the Armed Services Committee. Since the senior senator from Maine had taken over the post of chairman, things had been doubly rough. Dillman may have had a liking for scotch but he also had a love for human beings. Right now it was two against two: the president and Sherman versus Dillman and Jackson. And Dillman had it over them all in physical weight.

"Mr. President, the Indians are not trying to expand their perimeter, sir." Colonel Jackson watched the general out of the corner of his eye. "We can't just gun down those boys on ponies, and we can't use bombs because some of our civilian population is still within that area . . . ."

"Oh, hell!"

"Let him finish, General."

"Thank you, Mr. President." Jackson almost grinned at Sherman's discomfort. "Besides, sir, the Sioux now have three Minuteman silos in their control."

"Christ! Can they use those things, General? What would they do?" The president was afraid he knew.

"Ah . . . well, sir, they could get Chicago or Boston, maybe New York, but hell, we could wipe them out!"

The president paled. Dillman looked completely disgusted. "General, you must be related to Custer."

"Why you . . . !"

The president's intercom buzzed. "Yes?"

"Mr. Whitefish is here, sir."

"I'll deal with him in a few minutes." The president's head was killing him. "O.K., Senator, you've made your point. We can't move until this situation develops a more defined profile. You, General, will contain the Indians and that's all! No grandstand plays. Understood?"

"Yes, Mr. President." The general glared at Dillman. Dillman sipped his drink.

"Besides, unless we're forced to, it wouldn't sit well

with the UN to wipe out, as you put it, half a million Indians."

After dismissing one and all, the president considered the fact that the only Indians he had captured were Ed Small Wolf and his wife, Susan. At that point, Azile Whitefish was shown in. The president motioned him to a chair.

Whitefish sat across the desk from the man with a splitting headache, studying the palm of his hand. He was wondering just where in his lifeline he could find total ruin.

"Mr. Whitefish, you're an Osage?" The words hurt the chief executive's head.

"Sir?"

"I said, you are an Osage, aren't you? Just a moment." The president hit the intercom button. "Get me something in here for this damn headache . . . . O.K., now, Mr. Whitefish."

"Yes sir, Mr. President, full-blood."

"That's great, just wonderful. I wish I could say I was full-blood something or other." The president took the tablets offered by an aide and drained a glass of water. "Coffee, please. Now, Mr. Whitefish, had a man in here this while back. Full-blood Sioux. You know Congressman Small Wolf?"

"Yes sir, in a way. We have had some discussion concerning land grants and treaties." Mr. Whitefish wondered where this was heading.

"Well, now, Mr. Whitefish, I believe the question of

land and treaties has taken on a new complexion." The heavy brows came together. "You might say the Sioux have answered the question for themselves. Which brings us to why I asked you here."

The BIA director accepted the cup of coffee offered by the president's aide and did his damnedest not to spill it on himself. He managed to transfer it to a small table beside his chair and bravely undertook the task of lighting a cigarette. Shaking as he was, self-immolation was a real danger.

Obviously enjoying the man's discomfort, the president slowly stirred his coffee with cream and sugar and just a touch of Irish whiskey. Years of political training had given him an appetite for the kill. He got a kick out of watching men squirm as the man across his desk was doing just then.

It may not have encouraged Whitefish to know that two hours earlier his boss, the secretary of the interior, had gone through the same ordeal. The now former secretary of the interior was at that moment on his way back to Louisville, Kentucky. The president was doing his best to make up for a very bad day. When in doubt, throw 'em all out.

"Mr. Whitefish, it would be interesting to know why none of your people got wind of this Indian revolt before it got out of hand. Didn't you have any idea of what was going on?" The president leaned back and sipped his coffee. "Weren't you aware of the world-wide repercussions such things trigger? Or were you just plain uninterested?"

"Mr. President." Director Whitefish was attempting to put his cigarette into an ashtray, but he made it only as far as the rim of his coffee cup. The damp ashes did little to improve his composure. " . . . er . . . Mr. President, all that I was aware of was sent on to the secretary of interior. There really wasn't much . . . . "

"Yes, I have been informed of your messages to him. Now you can write it out in your report to me." The president leaned forward with a glint in his eyes. "That will be your last official duty. Since there aren't enough peaceful Indians left to make up a baseball team, we no longer require a Bureau of Indian Affairs. You know what that means, Mr. Whitefish? No Indians, no Bureau of Indian Affairs, and of course, no director. I'm afraid you're out of a job. Good night, sir!"

Mr. Whitefish made his exit. He had found that line he was looking for in the palm of his hand.

The president smiled and finished his coffee, trying to recall if there had been any Indians on the enemies list that had created such a stir a few years before. There certainly would be now.

Ottawa, Ontario, Canada . . . July 6, 1976—8:00 A.M.

"It doesn't matter one hill of beans to me what the United States is doing! We have to do something now, *right* now, before the UN gets into this." Canada's minister of national defense was extremely upset.

"These Mohawks have fired on Canadian officers. They have closed our seaway. What are we waiting for —for them to take over the rest of the country?" White knuckles bridged his clenched fist.

"I tell you that the United States will fool around until it's too late. They should have taken some action by now. They'll be forced to use a full-scale invasion force to clear up this mess, and they can't fight two wars anymore. That, gentlemen, means," he pounded emphasis on the long conference table, "we must act now to stop them right here!"

"What about the treaty, Parks?" the prime minister asked in an even voice. "The treaty that these people say we have violated is not written in sand. It won't just go away. True, we've never worried about it before, but this situation is a little different, wouldn't you say?"

"No, Mr. Prime Minister!" The minister of national defense jumped to his feet. "Civil war is what this is. Civil war! I don't give a damn what any treaty says!"

The prime minister's face grew red. "Now just a minute. Is this civil war? Are you so damn certain it could be called civil war?" He leaned forward, thin hands spread on the table. "If, in fact, we face the same problem the U.S. does, why haven't they moved sooner?" No answer.

"I'll tell you why." The prime minister felt certain of his ground. "They can't be sure either, that's why! Are tribes just tribes or are they nations? Do they have sovereign rights or no rights at all as nations? What rights do they have as Indians? Can you answer that?" His eyes were spitting fire. "Have we violated their rights? I tell you, sir, as I have told Parliament for the past five years: We had better correct our position, and we had better do it quick. Those Indians have not moved on a whim. They have waited a hundred years and you can bet your life they know what they're doing. They have bet theirs."

The minister of national defense sat down, staring blackly at the strained features of the prime minister. A year of fighting a lingering illness and the threat of a nervous breakdown had taken its toll on Prime Minister Dupré. The burdens of office caused setback after setback; the fragile state of his health was no secret to his allies and opponents alike. His political position was as fragile as his health, if not more so; and pressure for a general election was mounting from all sides. Fear of that eventuality was draining his remaining strength with frightening speed. The hounds hard on his heels were well aware of this effect and pressed all the harder as they smelled blood. Dupré was leaning on the few allies he had left, but even his own cabinet was shakily balanced. His efforts to introduce a new and fresh strain of thought into government dealings on Indian matters had met with one defeat after another. Criticism pointing to the fact that his wife was Mohawk had caused him no end of personal anguish. Try as he might, he had not always been able to protect her and the children from the barbs hurled their way.

It had been said that he was more interested in old treaties than in modern problems. The idea that the Canadian Indian was as entitled to national attention as was the French Separatist had never quite gotten off the ground. Up until now, the Indian had done nothing to gain attention beyond stepping in front of a police bullet from time to time. Compared to the overt actions of the separatist group, that was not enough to arouse public recognition of their struggle. In fact, a dead Indian was perfectly welcome in many parts of that so-called democratic nation. Over the years, the RCMP had done its best to provide enough dead Indians to satisfy the public. Not too many, just enough.

"It may do well, Mr. Parks, if you consider the rest

of the Indian population." The prime minister's tired eyes searched Parks' face. "How are you going to march into St. Regis and control all the western reserves at the same time?" A thin smile appeared on his pale lips. "Have you ever asked one of those western Indians how he felt about our seat of government? Since you make no apologies for the way you feel about Indians, I believe you should be aware that they hold no great love for us. The honeymoon ended around 1700. I fear your table-pounding will not impress them as much as you would like. With enough provocation, they may well burn your table, and I seriously don't believe you have the proper experience to control this situation without drastic, and perhaps tragic, results." The prime minister appeared to relax a bit.

"Are you prepared to accept the consequences of such force as you desire to direct at these people? A body count, sir, that is what your action would produce, a body count."

Ancient faces peered sightlessly from the paintings that covered the walls of the conference room. The silence of these figures from the past matched that of the men seated around the long, polished table. The discussion had run full circle and was once again at its starting point. For long moments it seemed no one was willing to try the track.

Knowing glances were exchanged between Parks and the minister of justice, who was seated opposite him. The graying gentleman had kept his own council up to that point, but it was he who now took up the gauntlet thrown down by the prime minister.

"Mr. Prime Minister." Minister of Justice Edmond Weston cast his cold gray eyes around the table. "Though you find Mr. Parks' solution somewhat distasteful, I feel it my duty to inform you that he is not alone in his desire to crush this action here and now. No one relishes the thought of body counts, but then, we have the rest of the people to consider."

It was obvious from the nods of agreement that the majority opposed the prime minister and his insistence that the treaties be considered a valid point in the action taken by the Mohawks. The prime minister directed his full attention to Mr. Weston.

"Am I then to understand, sir, that you would have me authorize the use of the RCMP in force against the Mohawks?"

"You understand me completely, Mr. Prime Minister." Weston folded his hands, content that he was in a position of advantage. "They are already in position at St. Regis."

"Then *you* understand *me*, sir! Such an order will not be issued until this government makes an effort to settle this in a civil, humane manner! Containment of the situation is one thing; but open warfare will not be tolerated as long as I sit at the head of this government." Prime Minister Dupré was clearly tired.

"Gentlemen, we will take a recess until the mood of this cabinet has tempered itself."

Within two hours of Dupré's dismissal of his cabinet, another meeting was under way in the office of the minister of justice. Dupré had lost ground and was not likely to gain it back under present conditions. Plans had to be made before the prime minister did something his colleagues considered drastic.

"It is not, I believe, impossible that Dupré will lose total control of this situation." The minister of justice sat in his large chair behind an ornate hand-carved desk. "I, for one, feel it is time we took more control. He has been swayed, no doubt, by his personal feelings for his wife's people. Those feelings have been a thorn in our side for some time. Those damn Mohawks must be stopped!" His pinkish features flushed slightly. "Bloody Indians!"

"All right, Weston. It is agreed action must be taken. All of us here feel that the P.M. is not acting in the best interest of our country." What Parks was really saying was that Dupré's hesitation was not in the best interest of those in the cabinet who opposed him. "It's beyond my understanding how he can let that rabble seize part of this country and do nothing but talk of those damn worthless treaties!"

"It remains only to determine what that action must be." Weston sipped his coffee and lit a cigarette in a slow, deliberate motion. He was feeling a surge of power as he measured the words he was about to speak.

"We must not let those Indians hold their ground. We have a very volatile situation on our hands. It would be most unfortunate, would it not, if an incident were provoked." Weston glanced at Parks who returned a nod.

A smallish man peered from behind thick glasses and adjusted himself in his chair. Minister of Forestry and Rural Development Howard Jamision Townsend had a smile on his thin lips. "It is my opinion, gentlemen, that the Mohawks could not have acquired the necessary equipment to create a real threat.... We have the RCMP in position. Heavy equipment would be a waste of time."

"Agreed." Weston answered. "No need to involve the armed forces in this. My people should be more than able to handle any, er, potential problem." The room was quiet for a moment.

"It is up to us, gentlemen . . . . " Weston cleared his throat meaningfully. "In the absence of decisive leadership, those with a sense of responsibility to the commonwealth at large must come to the fore." Weston poured himself another coffee and offered it up.

"Gentlemen, to our success . . . . " A smirk appeared on his pinkish face. "And to the Canadian people!"

*United Nations, General Assembly—New York City
. . . July 6, 1976—10:00 A.M.*

The small man adjusted the microphone on the podium. His fine brown hands moved to the papers lying before him and made busy adjustments to the order in which they lay. His face revealed pleasant thoughts and the large black eyes gave the impression of deep strength. He looked up, viewed the large room which stretched before him, and with sure confidence, he spoke.

"Mr. Secretary General; delegates and ambassadors; member nations: You here today are to be present at the birth of a nation . . . a nation born of five hundred years of suffering, five hundred years of strife, five hundred years of inhuman injustice on this North American continent.

"My country, the Republic of India, knows only too well the pain of their struggle and the depth of human sorrow they have endured. It is with honor and humility that we accept the privilege to present to the nations of the world their manifesto. They, too, are called Indian. For me, it is an honor—for them, an injustice. They choose to call themselves Anishinabe. They have paid a grave price, and they have earned the right to their name. Anishinabe!

"My government recognizes this right. We have given them our support in spirit and now . . . we openly . . . before all nations, give our support in fact. We urge all nations of the world to recognize the sovereign rights of the Anishinabe nation. We ask that the Anishinabe-waki Democracy take its place within the brotherhood of nations.

"Let us look, my friends, at the people of this new nation. Let us take a moment to find cause and purpose in their action.

"For most of us who have troubled to read the written history of the European conquest of North America, the American Indian, so called by the Europeans, appears as a naked savage, a child of nature. If we accept this concept, we may be excused from further examination and be content with the Anglo-European view of history which, simply put, says that the conquest of these people and their land was part of the natural progression of civilized man—civilized white man, that is. In this view, all that has occurred since that first conquest has been the fruit of progress and has worked for the greater good.

"Since we all here believe ourselves to be civilized, we may be excused for accepting this concept as it has applied to the native people of North America for five hundred years. But if we do, my fellow civilized men, we also must accept the less excusable contention that these same native people suddenly popped right out of the ground in order to assist the first white settlers in making their homes in what was a vast wilderness. If we follow this line of thinking, we must believe that it was part of the manifest destiny that these natives then disappear so these fine pioneers could get on with the business of progress, of raping that wilderness without interference from the red men who might try to protect their homes, their families, their very existence.

"But, to the great disappointment of the newcomers, the red man did not disappear. He did not know that he was dispensable in terms of the eternal plan of civilized man. The early settlers, however, understood progress to mean that once the knowledge of how to live on the continent was gained, civilization's next task would be to rid itself of the red man, an obstacle to progress and expansion.

"The native had been friendly and helpful, but his time had passed. Mankind had progressed beyond that primitive state and was compelled to contain and eliminate the savage Indian.

"What the Anglo-European pioneer did not understand and what the 'civilized' world as a whole has ignored is that the native American did not and does not exist simply as an early link in the chain of progress, to teach the European how to plant corn. He exists on his own terms; his people have been destined to live and thrive with this land, as they have, not for five hundred years, but for at least twenty thousand years of human experience, of human triumph and failure. His history is much the same as that of men all over the world. It is the basic human struggle to attain a oneness within himself and in the eyes of the Creator.

"This land, so proudly proclaimed the birthplace of freedom, has known the touch of the native American, and its soil has tasted his blood. Its forests and rivers, its mountains and plains, have been part of his body, his thought, his religion, his birth, his death. The spirit of this land is intermingled with the spirit of these people—the two are one and cannot be separated by logic or land grants which bear the seal of alien kings; nor could it be done by five hundred years of unjust treatment.

"In truth, the American wilderness did not exist until the white man came to this land. The native American found no wilderness here. He found oneness with nature's own plan. He grew and developed in the folds of her valleys. He lived and died in the softness of the vast forest which once covered this land. Within the context of nature and those gifts the Creator had placed at his disposal, the native American wove his culture to enhance his mind, his body, his soul. He did not destroy the work of those natural forces of which he was so much a part. But the beauty and dignity of native American culture was no match for European guns and greed.

"We do not say that all was purity and light here.

There was, as there is always, the bad as well as the good. But the good was plowed under in the white man's desperate grab for this rich and beautiful land. And the bad was used to justify the destruction of men, women, and children and all that they held dear.

"For five hundred cruel years, from the deliberate introduction of smallpox in the 1600s to the slaughter of starving Sioux at Wounded Knee Creek in 1890, the systematic destruction was carried out on his continent. The Anishinabe have trod a trail knee-deep in the blood of their own people and have been subjected to one of the most thorough and inhuman chapters of cultural genocide in the history of mankind.

"The trust they placed in the government of the United States has been rewarded with over four hundred broken treaties. These treaties were made, not with honorable intentions, but with the knowledge that they could and would be broken. This has been admitted by the very statesmen who wrote them. These treaties were a violation not only of human trust but of international law as well.

"What followed was the continual and open invasion of Anishinabe nations—not Indian tribes, but nations, nations, not by Indian tribal law, but by the very law of the United States. And, by the very same law of the United States, this present act of liberation, this so-called rebellion, is justified. The unlawful and continued transgressions by the United States on Anishinabe lands is no less to be condemned than were those transgressions which inspired the liberation of the United States itself. Independence of the United States justified rebellion against unjust governments. The Constitution of the United States, framed but a short time ago in relation to the history of civilization on this continent, did, in fact, have its origin in the League of the Iroquois, a confederacy nearly seven hundred years older than the United States.

"This international body may not be concerned with the beauty embodied in the ways of the Anishinabe nor with the preservation of those ways, but we are and must always be concerned with the human struggle for freedom.

"Anishinabe-waki has the right to freedom. Not even the United States, in all her power and glory, has the right to deny that freedom. The Anishinabe have taken nothing that is not rightfully theirs. They are making an effort to hold only what has been left to them. The courage and words of the leaders of the Anishinabe are not lessened by efforts to bury them under the heap of propaganda which America has developed in order to sweeten the sour stench left in the wake of bloody conquest. The words live on to inspire and enrich all who find them. I take pride in closing with the words of one such man.

"Thayandanega, known to the white man as Joseph Brandt, was of the Mohawk nation. On April 21, 1794, he spoke for his people, addressing himself to the United States and Great Britain. His text could have been written this morning, it is that pertinent to the present time, and I have chosen those words which lie close to the heart of the matter at hand. Thayandanega plainly does not fear war, but like his people today, asks only for freedom and the right to live as a free man in peace. Listen.

" 'Brothers! You, of the United States, listen to what we are going to say to you; you, likewise, the King.

" 'Brother: We are of the same opinion with the people of the United States; you consider yourselves as independent people; we, as the original inhabitants of this country and sovereigns of the soil, look upon ourselves as equally independent, and free as any other nation or nations. This country was given to us by the Great Spirit above; we wish to enjoy it, and have our passage along the lake, within the line we have pointed out.

" 'Brother: The great exertions we have made, for this number of years, to accomplish a peace, and have not been able to obtain it; our patience, as we have already observed, is exhausted, and we are discouraged from persevering any longer. We, therefore, throw ourselves under the protection of the Great Spirit above who, we hope, will order all things for the best. We have told you our patience is worn out; but not so far, but that we wish for peace, and whenever we hear that pleasing sound, we shall pay attention to it.' "

As he spoke, the quiet of the large room was such that the small brown man could have been alone. But when he spoke those words and then himself fell silent, the room burst into a noisy chaos. Shouts of "Freedom!" and "Viva Anishinabe!" in delegation after delegation rang in the ears of the honorable ambassador of the United States of America. His discomfort was shared by his fellows from Canada. The wish to be someplace else had taken on an international flavor.

This unpleasant moment for the United States was not lessened as the six-man Executive Council of Anishinabe-waki was escorted into the assembly hall and seated with the Indian delegation. As is customary among ambassadors to the UN, the Anishinabe were wearing the traditional dress of their nations. Since each man was of a different nation—this new nation united all native American nations—the variety and color added to the impact of their entrance. Lakota, Navajo, Pueblo, Mohawk, Hopi, Cheyenne—the Anishinabe stood proudly before the world community.

The gavel of the secretary general sounded again and again. "Vote! Vote!" rang throughout the hall. It took quite a few minutes before the air was calm enough to enable the small man at the podium to continue. He had stood easily during the demonstration, smiling and nodding to each man as he assumed his seat in his country's delegation.

It goes without saying that it was more than simply the idea of freedom for Anishinabe-waki that had set those honorable men to chanting like kids at a football game. An opportunity to embarrass the United States had more than a little to do with it. The Russian ambassador had been so elated that he ripped the back of his coat while waving his arms, and broke off the jack to his headset.

Freedom is nice, but blood is better. How utterly civilized the nations of the world had become. Of course, for the Anishinabe-waki, it was better to be part of civilization than to be under its heel. The reaction had been counted on and the Executive Council was obviously very pleased.

"India . . . " the speaker had to hesitate once more to wait for silence. "India stands with these people, this nation, as its friend, its ally, its brother. India will stand against all who oppose the rights of these people, their sovereignty, their freedom. It is the request of my country that the manifesto of this new nation be read into the annals of the United Nations . . . . "

The Indian Ambassador was again drowned out by a burst of applause and an uncontrolled demonstration of support for the new nation.

When silence again reigned, the manifesto of the Anishinabe-waki became part of the record of the United Nations.

Akwesasne . . . July 6, 1976—Late evening

A bullet tore through the door of the old car. Seconds later, another barrage ripped gaping holes that ran in a jagged line from front to rear fender. The driver spilled out the safe-side door. He had barely gained his feet when the deadly rattle reached and ignited the auto's gas tank. He felt a blast of heat on his back as he raced toward a sand-bagged bunker twenty yards away.

The darkness was punctuated by the rising and falling flames of burning gasoline. The man's feet read the ground as his eyes absorbed the macabre scene in the flickering half-light before him. He knelt to touch a boy who lay in his path, his unfired rifle jammed under his chest. He was dead, his entire face ripped away. After a word to the boy's spirit in his own language, Jesse was on his feet again, moving toward the bunker.

His hair streaming like a black contrail, he took to the air for the final five yards as he desperately tried to outdistance the sputter of gunfire tracing his path.

Sand still dribbled from smoking holes in the bunker as Jesse Hood shook the haze from his eyes. Someone had built the bunker too damn narrow and Jesse had tried to correct the error with his head.

"Just what the hell started this?" Jesse had to scream above the burst from an automatic rifle. Then it was quiet.

Three figures sat on their heels, backs against the wall.

"Don't know, Jess. Before we knew it, they got Bill. He never knew what hit him. We thought it was the UN but then they opened up." The man fingered the beads at his throat. "Guess they're RCMP, huh?"

"Yeah, they're somebody." Jesse slowly surveyed the area through the slit window in the front wall above the three men. "Any idea what they got?"

"Just automatic rifles so far."

Jesse dropped below the slit as three flashes stitched the road fifty yards away. Another three flashes followed seconds later.

"Damn! Took those guys long enough to get outta bed!"

The guns were silent for a minute, then repeated their message.

"Them mortars were probably a piece of news the RC's coulda done without." Pete LaNose fingered his beads.

"Bastards! What the hell are they try'n to prove? Shooting's supposed to be over!"

Jesse checked his weapon. "In about five minutes they'll wish to their God it *was* over." The Mohawk picked up the movement in the wooded areas to the rear. "Think maybe we're about to get some of Canada back."

The whine of incoming mortar fire sounded up the road while dark shrouded figures moved silently past the bunker. A head appeared at the entrance.

"Jesse still in that car out there?"

"No, in here, Tommy."

Tommy Hood slid into the bunker. "Man! Thought you'd bought it, big brother. Saw the boom but didn't see you get out. Guess they ruined our car, huh?" Jesse laughed.

"Yeah! Your favorite back-seat motel ain't no more!" The old '59 Pontiac had been with them awhile. The brothers had shared it as they did most everything else, including some of the motel guests.

"O.K." Jesse started out past the four men. "Let's go. Those boys are walk'n that mortar up the road. Let's get with it." They joined the Mohawk troops moving toward the edge of the reserve.

The mist-filled dawn broke on new territory for the Mohawks. The all-night fight had indeed returned sixteen square miles of Canada to its original owners. But it had cost, on both sides. The price littered the partially wooded area in a crazy-quilt pattern that traced the path of the battle from the bunker to the present line of Mohawks who now held their position without any further opposition from the RCMP forces. Medics were checking the dead and assisting the more seriously wounded who hadn't been able to move themselves during the night. Jesse and Tommy Hood headed back to find some fresh coffee. They paused to take a look at the smoking hulk of their former traveling companion. Mortar crews and a mobile missile launcher moved past the charred Pontiac to position in line with the new perimeter.

"Looks awful sad, don't she?" Tommy picked up a handful of dirt and tossed it at the twisted metal. The two men turned and went on.

"Ya know, Jesse, I can't figure why they did this. Hell, what could they hope to gain? The UN already put a hold on positions. They knew they couldn't cross the river anyway 'cause the U.S. wasn't about to get into it." The young Mohawk watched a truck filled with wounded pass. "Look at that . . . . For what?"

"Tommy, we knew we could all get sent on in this and we took that chance. But you're right. Don't seem to prove nothing right now." Jesse lit a smoke and offered the pack to his brother. "Damn fool Canucks! Guess maybe they just like shoot'n red niggers. This time it cost them, though. Hope to hell it was worth it to him." Jesse pointed to a stretcher with the body of an olive-jacketed Canadian on it. "Wonder what his family will think?"

"Price is a little high for red niggers, I'd guess." Tommy handed the pack of butts back to Jesse. "They can't even get a good price for our scalps anymore!"

"My guess is that somebody made a bad mistake.

Don't have any use for them RC's but I'm sure they could have made a better fight of it if it'd been planned." Jesse shook his head. "Just a goddamn stupid mistake!"

*Office of the Prime Minister—Ottawa, Ontario, Canada
. . . July 7, 1976—1:55 P.M.*

"Stupid mistake? Stupid mistake! Is that what I tell the country? A stupid mistake! Is that how I explain to my wife that we killed fifteen of her people at St. Regis? Oh my God . . . . "

The prime minister sat with his face buried in his hands. A crumpled report of the RCMP action lay at his feet. He lifted his head, the tired, drawn features almost screaming under the strain of sleepless nights. The distress was reflected in his voice as he spoke.

"Do you suggest I wire all the families of those troopers killed and advise them that they died of a 'stupid mistake'? What the hell are you trying to do? Start your own Viet Nam?"

The questions was directed at the minister of justice but it received no answer. The prime minister's red-rimmed eyes searched the man's face for a sign of understanding, for some indication of real concern. He found none.

"Sir! We have lost forty-three men. Men, goddamn

it. Not just uniforms, *men!* We have killed fifteen Mohawk people. People, not just numbers on your goddamn records, not just red niggers, but flesh-and-blood *people.* And that could have been women and children for all I know! For what?" The prime minister's voice broke. "For what? A body count . . . . "

His chief aide stepped forward.

"Mr. Prime Minister, are you all right, sir?" He poured a glass of water from the service on the desk and offered it.

"Get me some brandy, please," the prime minister said slowly, pushing aside the glass of water.

"When this reaches the western reserves, we'll have a full-scale civil uprising on our hands. There isn't an Indian in Canada who won't be out for blood. And by God, we asked for it." The brandy came and was swiftly drained.

"Along with the French Separatist actions, I seriously doubt this government or the country will be able to take this."

He forced himself out of the chair to walk around, his fifty-two years sitting heavily on his slumped shoulders. Flashes of his wife's face and those of her family streamed before his mind's eye. He had failed in all his efforts for her people and was now indirectly responsible for the supreme failure: open warfare. Or was it murder? It was hard to tell what the UN would determine to call it. War, murder, genocide, civil uprising—it didn't matter. The fact remained that Canada, in all her splendor, had fought a battle within her own borders and lost. Thoughts struggled for his attention as he tried to gain control of his racing mind. The murmur of the men present reverberated in his ears like drums.

"Gentlemen." The prime minister strained to maintain his composure. "Gentlemen, twenty minutes ago the French Separatists in Quebec declared a state of independence. Your action has seriously weakened our position. We have no recourse at this point but to wait. Our strength has been expended in a foolhardy action that cost lives and time. You are fools." He paused and picked up a paper from his desk.

"This is a statement from the new independent nation of French Quebec. I quote: 'A state of independence now exists in French Quebec. We, the free and independent people of Quebec, will defend our nation with all our resources and to the very death, if necessary. We hereby disavow any allegiance to the nation of Canada or its government.' End quote. They didn't bother to sign it."

The prime minister sat down. "Well, which way do we go now? Which one of you can answer that? In a matter of days, you have destroyed this country. Behind my back, you gave orders which will virtually shatter this nation. Your grasping search for power, your racism, your utter failure to consider the result of your actions have done more to destroy our country than either Mohawks or the French!" The strained features of the prime minister revealed the expenditure of his waning strength.

"I will dissolve this cabinet and all of you must answer for that. God only knows what you have done. Canada will never forgive you. Perhaps . . . . " His voice broke.

Rupturing the uneasy silence, all the men began to speak at once, each voicing his disinclination to take the blame for what they claimed was the prime minister's own failure. The broken man did not defend himself; he personally felt the truth of their accusation.

"Quiet! I need quiet!" He turned on those in the room in a rage. "Get out of here and let me think!"

The room cleared as if a plug had been pulled. The last man out was his chief aide.

"Mr. Prime Minister," he spoke softly. "Sir, why not try to rest for awhile?"

"Thanks, Jean. Soon . . . soon . . . perhaps . . . . " His voice trailed off, lost in despair. The aide quietly closed the door.

The moments passed as Prime Minister Dupré absently paced back and forth across his office. Confused pictures of disjointed discussions darted in and out of his brain: brief scenes of days spent at St. Regis with his wife; fights in the cabinet on Indian rights. Nothing stayed in place long enough for him to grasp its meaning. His government was lost and he knew there was nothing he could do now to save it, or himself as its leader. He had simply lost control of everything.

An hour passed. He paused, poured himself another brandy and drained the glass. He put down the glass and walked slowly to his desk. From the upper right-hand drawer he removed the silver-plated revolver given to him by the RCMP on their centennial in 1973. He carefully checked the chamber, clicked it shut; then the prime minister of Canada placed the barrel in his mouth and blew his brains out.

Oval Office of the President—Washington, D.C.
...July 7, 1976—5:45 P.M.

It could have been an instant replay: the president, General Sherman, Colonel Jackson, and, of course, Senator Keller Dillman, all seated as they had been not a few hours earlier. The situation had changed drastically, however. At the moment, the room was silent but for the sound of ice clinking in Dillman's glass. The senator was never late but he insisted that his glass be ready when he arrived. He had been known to leave if it wasn't.

"Gentlemen." The president's voice was taut as he broke the silence of several minutes. "Gentlemen, the United Nations has now, as I'm sure you are aware, taken an active hand in our internal, er, affairs. India has made it an international matter." His face was grim as he stared at the paper in front of him.

"Also, I've just learned that the prime minister of Canada is dead by his own hand. As you know, his forces took a nasty whipping at St. Regis. He was under great pressure. It must have been too much for him."

The silence was thick. At the click of the intercom, a steward entered and occupied the empty moments by serving coffee and drinks, leaving each man in the room to his own thoughts.

It was finally Dillman who raised his glass. "To Dupré; he gave it his all." His toast was not well received.

"Senator."

"Yes, Mr. President?"

"He was a good man."

"I'm sure. And that's just what I meant. If you're a good man, you give it everything you've got. With me, it's my liver." Colonel Jackson did his best not to laugh.

"The fact remains, gentlemen, that we must now attempt to deal . . . " The word stuck in the president's throat. " . . . deal with that rabble."

"Mr. President, they are not rabble," Dillman reminded him. "They are Indians, or Nishnabe, as they wish to be called." Dillman shifted his huge body. "Right or wrong, they are still people. Even that racist bastard, Thomas Jefferson, was human. Would you call him rabble? He did the same thing." Again, Jackson stifled a smile. Dillman continued.

"It isn't going to be easy to 'deal' with them either. I'm sure they haven't forgotten how the white man made deals before: a bunch of junk traded for vast tracts of land. Then we took what they didn't want to trade, and we didn't take it nicely, not at all. God! Deal? Mr. President, would you care to 'deal' with people like us? We dealt with them all right—at the end of a gun." Dillman had a faraway look in his eyes.

" 'As long as the grass grows and the river flows . . . etc., etc., etc!' Mr. President, how do you 'deal' with a people you've lied to and murdered for five hundred years? I think they'd rather have smallpox than our promises. We gave them both and it's hard to say which was more deadly!" The senator took a large belt of scotch.

"If we get cornered into trying to make all those old treaties good, we'll end up with Plymouth Rock, and damn lucky to hold that!"

The air of discomfort was cut suddenly by the buzz of the red telephone on the president's desk. Each man in the room knew what it meant and even the president hesitated for a moment before he answered it.

"Yes? . . . Yes . . . . Yes, Mr. Chairman . . . . Yes, Mr. Chairman . . . . You will have our full cooperation, Mr. Chairman. Good-bye." He replaced the receiver.

"Shit!" Like a dog that had just been kicked, he looked at Sherman.

"General, there will be overflights to the Indian states by aircraft of the USSR, India, Ghana, Sweden, France . . . . Oh hell! And almost every other country in Europe. I have just been reminded that, according to that damn Arab-Israeli Pact we signed in Geneva in December of '75, such 'peace' flights are allowed. You'd better make damn sure no one . . . *no one* fires on them. You're excused." Sherman's face dropped three feet.

"But . . . but, how?"

"Just do it, damn it!" General Sherman saluted stiffly and, just as stiffly, took his leave.

The president's gaze nailed itself on Jackson. "Colonel, I understand you and Congressman Small Wolf are friends."

"Yes, sir."

"Do you think he'll help us?"

"No, sir." The answer was sharp and direct.

"Well, in any case, Colonel Jackson, you are going to find out, *now!*"

"Yes, Mr. President."

"And you, Senator, finish your drink and get the hell out of here! My whole damn strategy has just been blown all to hell!"

Dillman downed the scotch. "King George must have felt that way once, Mr. President. You're in good company. Good night, sir."

Bethesda, Maryland . . . July 7, 1976—8:40 P.M.

"It doesn't really matter what you think, Colonel Jackson!" Congressman Small Wolf's voice had begun to rise.

"What the hell's this 'Colonel' shit? Just because you're pissed off at the whole damn country doesn't mean you've got to get formal with me. Hell, I can't come out and say it, but you know how I feel, Ed." Col. Harold Jackson gulped down the last of his coffee and tried to collect his thoughts.

"Ed, they sent me here to see what your position was. Talks with your people aren't going to be easy. The president has had second thoughts and feels you'd be valuable as a middleman and. . . . "

"A middleman?" Ed was shouting now. "You can tell your president that I'm not in the middle. I'm a prisoner of war! Susan and I want to go home and if we can't, we expect to be treated as POWs! Don't come around with this crap about talking for your government!"

"Now slow down, Ed." Col. Jackson was grappling for a foothold against Small Wolf's torrent of words. "You know I have to follow orders and my orders are simply to ask you if you will act as a neutral representative . . . ."

"Oh, for Christ's sake, Harold! You've done your duty and you know damn well what the answer is! Damn it to hell, I'm an Indian, not neutral! Indian! As far as I'm concerned, you and I no longer live in the same country. The Sioux nation is part of Anishinabewaki, and I am of the Sioux nation. Clear enough? Or do I have to take what is left of your kinky little scalp to prove it?" Jackson grinned and rubbed a hand across his balding head of short black hair.

"Now wait just a minute, you heathen! It may be kinky, but I'm still very attached to it! You're right, these questions are asinine. I knew it when they sent me over here but it's still my country, even if it isn't yours." He laid aside the sheaf of papers he had been holding and spoke seriously.

"Off the record . . . and try to hold it down, will you? That M.P. outside the door isn't as dumb as he looks, brass buttons notwithstanding." Col. Jackson paused and looked at his friend intently. "Ed, did you know this was going to happen?"

"I am ashamed to say that I didn't." Susan entered the room and refilled the coffee cups. Her presence made the tension drain away. "Apparently, Hal, my people feel I'm a middleman, too. Not red, not white —kinda pink. This whole mess has forced me to think about a lot of things. For the first time since I was a kid in that damn BIA school, I've been reminded that I'm not and never could have been a real part of this country. They won't let you." A painful smile crossed his face. "I've got to tell *you* that?"

Hurt showed in the black man's eyes but he said nothing. Small Wolf continued.

"It's really weird. I've worked hard and almost had myself convinced that a lot of the old barriers were falling, that it didn't matter anymore. An Indian or a black man could really accomplish something. But it's the goddamn system. You just can't be part of a system that's alien to what you are, and the basic part of this system will never change. It's lily-white and they have never, nor do they ever intend to, let it be tinted by any color, be it red, black, or brown."

"Perhaps . . . . " It was obvious Hal didn't fully agree. "But Ed, all your people don't feel that way. We know now that there are quite a large number of non-reservation Indians who don't buy this war. What about them?"

"Frankly, I don't give a damn about them. Being Indian is more than having your name on an agency roll." Ed leaned forward. "I assume you've met Azile Whitefish? There's been a vast misconception of just what being Indian is, ever since we adopted the white man's edict that the skin and not the heart makes a man what he is. Mr. Whitefish is a number one, prime example.

"Whitefish is full-blood and is entitled to certain 'rights.' Half-bloods and quarter-bloods get proportionately less. It doesn't matter if the quarter-blood lives in a hogan in the middle of Navajo land—excuse me, Cabolclo—he still is not as 'Indian' as Whitefish. Of all the things we've picked up from the white man, only smallpox has caused more trouble and heartache." As an afterthought, he said softly, "And I'm a full-blood, too . . . according to the roll."

Ed stood up and walked to the window. He gazed absently at nothing in particular, his mind working at remembering.

"The BIA has doled out land and money on the basis that one guy deserves more than the other because his daddy 'looked' Indian. Over the years, we just accepted it, and it has cost us many great men. Agency number! Christ! Only dogs and Indians need papers in this country to prove what they are, and dogs don't care." He turned with anger in his dark eyes.

"The truth is, Hal, most of the rolls have been tampered with anyway. They should have been shitcanned ages ago. Now those Indians on the rolls who don't want in on the conflict have got a real problem. If the government decides to treat them the way they treated the Japanese-Americans in World War II, it's going to be the Trail of Tears all over. Removal? They'll probably decide too late that they're really part of this after all. Either that or they'll cry great big tears that they are the 'good Indians.' Too late! The U.S. has literally got their number—their agency number!"

"Now, look, Ed! I hardly think the government would...."

"You don't *think?* Man, neither did those Nisei think they would end up in a concentration camp. Some of them couldn't believe it until the camp gate was closed on them!"

Ed decided something stronger than coffee was in order and asked Susan to fix them all a drink.

"Hal, just ask yourself why this congressman of the United States is under house arrest. Senator Glover is from South Dakota too, but is the good Senator Glover under house arrest? You can bet what's left of your little kinky scalp, he isn't. He's white!"

Oval Office of the President—Washington, D.C.
...July 7, 1976—10:38 P.M.

The president had been listening intently to the man across the desk. He looked puzzled. Finally, in desperation, he broke into the monologue.

"I'm sorry, General, but I've listened to you for the past fifteen minutes, and I know hardly more about this than when you started." He leaned forward and sipped his special blend of coffee.

"Now, if you will be kind enough, just explain what in blue blazes took place. Was it a confrontation? A fight? A mistake? And if there wasn't any fire fight as you say, how in the hell did we lose twenty-five men? Where was that UN observer? What happened to those three tanks?" He felt at a loss for words. "Now, I always suspected and am more convinced every minute that those damn Indians are clever, but this is beyond belief!"

"Mr. President, sir, it wasn't just the Indians this time. We could fight Indians...."

"General, may I remind you that the RCMP had

that idea, and it proved a stupid one. Who did we fight? The UN?"

The general let his eyes drop. "No, sir. Each other . . . sort of . . . . " The general didn't know quite how to finish, so he left it at that.

"Each other?" The president sat bolt upright. "What the hell do you mean, 'each other'?"

"Please, Mr. President, I'm trying to explain . . . . "

"Well, damn it all, man! Spit it out!"

"Well . . . eh . . . the sixty-seven men we've lost . . . . "

"Sixty-seven? I thought you said twenty-five!"

"I did." The general fumbled for words. "Twenty-five this morning. All together, sixty-seven . . . at last count. It could be less . . . or more." That last phrase was just barely audible.

"Were they killed, captured, or what?"

"Oh, they . . . . Actually, sir . . . they seem to have gone over to the Indians. Lock, stock, and combat boots!"

"You mean tanks, don't you?"

"Yes, yes, sir. Tanks . . . three of them." His eyes followed a line of type on the sheet of paper he held in his hand. He added, "and one jeep and two trucks . . . assorted small arms . . . . " The president was up and pacing.

"All right! All right! That's enough! Now, how the hell did it happen?"

The general decided not to ad-lib any longer and read directly from the report in his hand.

"With your permission, Mr. President . . . . At

twenty-two thirty hours, 'Charlie' Company reported sighting a group of civilians moving toward the Indian perimeter. They were passing close to an armored unit detached along a suspected weak point in our line of defense. The O.I.C. dispatched a patrol to stop and hold the group. Care was taken since the civilians appeared to be armed.

"On challenge, the leader of the civilian group offered to come forward alone and unarmed to speak with the NCO in charge of the patrol, one Sergeant Wallace Youngblood. The exact content of this discussion is not noted because the NCO in question is among the missing and presumed to have joined those who crossed into Indian-held territory.

"By twenty-three hundred hours, the group also included the NCO in charge of the armor detachment and several enlisted men assigned to that unit. From the position of the command post, a lengthy discussion appeared to take place during which time a UN observer, later known to be of the Czech contingent, joined the growing number of participants.

"At twenty-three forty-five hours, the NCO in charge radioed back a request that all units not directly attached to his own patrol and the armor unit hold their positions until further notice. His request was granted since no hostile action had been observed. With that, all those then in the area under command post observation crossed into Indian-held territory and disappeared—tanks, troops, trucks, jeeps, and one UN observer.

"The last radio message received by the command post read: 'Long live the spirit of Crazy Horse.' The report was signed: 'Lt. Col. H.J. Harland, S.D.N.G.' "

The general avoided the eyes of the president and relit his cigar, making more of an effort than was actually required. The president had another of his splitting headaches.

Several moments passed in silence, broken only by the snap of an asprin bottle the president had begun keeping in his desk. It had occurred to him that his headaches were becoming more frequent and that they usually began with the utterance of the word "Indian."

The president settled back in his chair, waiting for a refill of coffee and Irish whiskey. He looked at the general and the look clearly said "wish you weren't here." Then he began to speak, biting off his words as though he only reluctantly allowed them to pass his lips.

"All right, General, does that explain the twenty-five missing men or the whole sixty-seven?" He sipped his coffee and did his best to simply accept whatever his chief of staff had to say. The general swallowed the last of a double bourbon and chased it with coffee. He cleared his throat before bravely taking up the report once again.

"Actually, Mr. President, only the twenty-five." The president drained his cup in one gulp. "The other forty-two did the same thing but in smaller groups and a bit less boldly. At least, they left our tanks and equipment behind." He tried to laugh but straightened himself when he saw his joke had not carried. "What I mean is, they only took their personal weapons." Looking down again he added very softly, "And two mortars . . . . "

A deliberately controlled voice put in, "Was this all in South Dakota, General?"

"Er . . . no, Mr. President. Thirteen at the southwestern area and twenty-nine at St. Regis, the Mohawk area."

"General, between your report, a very nasty headache, too damn many asprins, and this whiskey, I find I don't feel well. You're dismissed for thirty minutes."

The president brushed aside the general's salute and watched sullenly as the closing door left him alone with his nausea. The president rose, crossed the room in two steps, and was quietly ill in his plush, personal, presidential washroom.

Akwesasne . . . July 7, 1976—Late evening

"I don't doubt that they're sincere. After all, 'white' Mohawks are nothing new."

The man spoke with firmness and the self-assurance of one who knew he would be listened to. "They are welcome and are to be made to feel welcome." Green eyes searched the room for any hint of disagreement. Finding none, they regained the softness usually present there.

"Clear them, house them, feed them, explain our cause to them. If they choose to remain they will be expected to fight as Anishinabe. If they do not wish to fight, they will be treated as POWs and not harmed. It is, then, as it always was."

2

"HAIL TO THE CHIEF" SOUNDS LIKE HELL ON DRUMS!

If the Great Spirit had desired me to be a white man, he would have made me so in the first place . . . . Each man is good in His sight. It is not necessary for eagles to be crows. Now we are poor, but we are free. No white man controls our footsteps. If we must die, we die defending our rights.

—SITTING BULL, HUNKPAPA LAKOTA

Cabolclo . . . August 15, 1976—Late afternoon

The routine of patrol had become part of everyday life for Joe Eddie Morris. The long summer had been dull and unusually hot even for the desert country. Joe Eddie had taken to leading his pony on foot when he was on duty in the afternoon, partly to rest them both from the heat and partly because he preferred walking anyway. Although he had been requested to do so three or four times, he hadn't given up his AR–15 for the .30/30 they told him to carry. He was stripped and painted for duty as ordered and little streaks of sweat ran rivers through the laugh lines on his face.

Except for those things that touched him personally, he wasn't really aware of all that had taken place in the past month. The heated interaction of international politics held little interest for him, especially after he met that Crow girl from up north. From that moment on, he just did what he was told and spent the rest of his time daydreaming about that pretty little thing called Twila. He was rip-roaring mad when he had been removed from guarding the chairman, because that post gave him the chance to see her at the agency center once in a while. Now he could see her only on off-duty hours and for him that was not enough.

Joe Eddie was kicking rocks and sand on every third step as he rounded a small bluff. His mind was elsewhere, and he didn't notice how close he was approaching the National Guard outpost. The first smack of bullets against the sand took time to register in his mind. He was jarred back to reality just in time to hear the rattle of an automatic weapon. His pony screamed, rearing wildly, his feet kicking air as lead ripped through his flanks, neck, and shoulders. A second burst caught him as he tossed backward, foam and blood streaming from his mouth and nostrils.

The reins jerked from Joe Eddie's hand, throwing him off balance. He pulled his AR–15 on target as he caught his footing. He was still firing moments later when he landed on his back, his chest a mass of torn flesh.

Three guardsmen had been watching as Joe Eddie strolled into view. Two of them still watched, not believing the scene they had just witnessed. They stared at the boy sprawled on the hot sand fifty yards in front of them, his chest now gleaming red in the sun. The third guardsman was climbing over the front of the bunker, pulling his bayonet from his scabbard as he went.

"Told you guys I'd get me one of them red bastards.

Now I'm gonna show 'em how to play cowboys and Indians for real."

Realizing that the Indian was dead, Cpl. Tom Johnson did his best to think rationally. "My God, you killed that kid," was all that came out. "You killed him . . . ."

"Right on, and now I'm going scalp 'im." Phil Dickson was running low, knife in hand, toward the boy's body. He was moving too fast for Johnson to reach him. "Told my old man I'd bring him a scalp!"

"You crazy son of a bitch! Leave him be!" Johnson screamed at the top of his lungs. He pulled his rifle up and fired. "Stop, goddamn you, or I blow your head off." He fired again just as a jeep bounced over the sand behind the dead Indian. One burst from the .50 caliber machine gun mounted on its rear robbed Dickson of his chance for personal glory. He was cut in half before he even knew he was being fired on.

Three Nishnabe troops hit the ground before the jeep had slid to a stop. The machine gunner ripped the National Guard bunker with a steady fire. It was obvious they could do nothing for Joe Eddie but they could make the guardsmen pay for his life. No orders were given. None were necessary.

Corporal Johnson was on his field phone begging for help. The sound of the fire fight had carried back to the field headquarters but nothing like this had happened before and things were in a ragged state of confusion.

"I don't know where they came from," he was

shouting, "but Christ, get us some help or they're gonna be all over us! They're moving...." The boy beside him groaned and went limp. A Nishnabe trooper landed with both feet on the edge of the bunker and ripped Johnson open with one blast from his weapon. The corporal's body was thrown backward, a look of surprise plastered on his face for eternity.

The trooper quickly backed away from the bunker and walked toward the jeep. Three for one. It was the old way.

Emil Tall Warrior turned from the body in the back of the jeep. He ran his hand through his hair and replaced his straw hat. He showed no emotion as he spoke in an even voice to the sergeant who had been Joe Eddie's backup.

"How did this happen, Sergeant? How far back were you?"

"Just over the ridge, Captain." The sergeant shook his head. "I don't know. Joe Eddie was a little close in, but hell, they never gave him a chance! By the time we could get there, it was too late." The Comanche kicked the dirt. "If we coulda done anything, we woulda but, Captain, they had him before he knew it." He glanced over at the covered body. "You ain't gonna believe this, but I think they were gonna take his hair. That one guy was headed for him with a knife. Man! He musta been off his rocker or somethin'!"

Tall Warrior was looking at the ground. "You say you killed all three of them?"

"Yes, sir." the sergeant was retying the red band around his head. "Once we got there and found the kid, it just seemed like the thing to do. Maybe we was wrong. Shoulda kept at least one alive. But it just happened so damn fast. Three or four minutes and it was all over."

"Yeah, don't imagine I'd have done much different, but now we won't ever know what really happened." The captain started for his jeep. "Take care of Joe Eddie, Sergeant. I believe we're gonna catch hell for this. Got to talk to the chairman."

By the time Tall Warrior had reached the office of the chairman he was hurt and mad. In an effort to ease the captain's strain, Art tried to turn his mind in another direction.

"Full alert is in effect now, Emil." Art Navarro eased back in his chair. "Not really sure what the U.S. will do about this."

"Hank, you're sure they knew about the backup on our sentry riders?" Tall Warrior's puzzlement was apparent as he looked at the vice-chairman, Hank Trujillo.

"Emil." Hank adjusted his straw hat. "You know as well as I do that their air recon picked that up on the second day of this little outing. It doesn't make sense that they wouldn't let their frontline people know, but maybe they slipped up."

"Well, from what Sergeant Yellow Horse told me, those guardsmen thought Joe Eddie was fair picking. One of them was trying to get to the body when the backup got there. If Joe Eddie had been one of those guys from the Movement, I'd say that he might have provoked this, but the kid wasn't that way. They had to have fired first!" The captain's personal feelings were beginning to show. "And where the hell was the UN? Off picking its nose, I guess."

The chairman poured himself some coffee.

"Take it easy, Emil. We know you liked the boy. The fact is, we don't know why they fired, but problems are going to develop just the same. Yellow Horse shouldn't have killed all those guardsmen."

"Damn it, Art, he didn't have time to do anything else." Captain Tall Warrior was trying to keep his temper under control. "The sergeant didn't know how far those people were going. For all he knew it could have been a full-scale assault. He just did his job and did it well. That unit he heads is tops, and he knows his business. The boys on his team were all trained in his outfit back in Oklahoma, so it wasn't a matter of their losing their heads under fire. Most of them saw combat in Vietnam. Sergeant Yellow Horse brought those boys a long way to join us here, and they didn't come out here to foul up. They just did what they were supposed to do."

"The fact remains that we've one dead and sure as hell we aren't going to get anywhere worrying about him. If the U.S. wants a fight, they're gonna get a good one."

Art's dark face reflected little of his inner turmoil. This was not what he wanted, not now. It was so

damn stupid to fight at this point. Yet the heavy rumble of tanks and trucks filled the agency center. The
entire state of Cabolclo was on the move. The security
perimeter around the chairman's office was tightened.
Alert and ready IPF men prepared to defend this
point as a last outpost if that became necessary. They
knew full well that if it came to that, it would be the
dying breath of their state. If the U.S. forces got as far
as headquarters the Nishnabe would be finished. Captain Tall Warrior adjusted his trousers and sighed
heavily.

"Art, the UN will do something, I'm sure of it!" He
slammed his fist on the desk. "Damn it! Where the hell
were they? Four men died while those bastards were
off sipping tea!"

"Yes." Art's voice was calm. "It appears they
haven't kept up on U.S. tactics. Wounded Knee's dead
should have taught them something. The U.S. talks
with two faces, and one of them spits bullets. That's
the one they talk to Indians with. The Movement may
have been a little ahead of itself at Wounded Knee, but
dead men are dead a long time. Those men that died
three years ago apparently didn't make much impression." He paused, and a look of pain clouded his eyes.

"Why? Why can't white men see that red men hurt
too? What was it Sitting Bull said? 'Why can't white
men act like like human beings?' "

◆   ◆   ◆

While the chairman had moved his forces to the alert and waited for the situation to unfold, the opposing United States troops were coming out of shock and assuming the appearance of soldiers. Men and their machines shook off their torpor and began the practiced maneuvers of advancing into battle. Armor and infantry moved together toward their assigned assault positions. As they advanced across the perimeter, past the National Guard outpost Corporal Johnson had recently occupied, a young private leaped to the rim of the bunker and looked inside. His face went ashen. Before he could control himself, the sight of the two men in the hole sent him into convulsions of retching.

Between gagging breaths, he managed to blurt out "medic" and was rocked again by the sight. "Oh, goddamn it, medic!" he screamed.

A medic ran up and quickly saw there was no need for his services in the bunker. He headed toward the body of Dickson, about thirty yards away, but there was little he could do there either. The medic was as green as the private. He wasted no time getting back to his unit, which was taking position along a line of attack.

The unit's hurried orders from headquarters had been to move in to forward positions and then hold. Since no one was sure of anything except that three men were dead, their commanding officer was reluctant to order an attack without backing from Washington. That word "overkill" was familiar to him. He had been in on one or two in Vietnam.

*Headquarters, Containment Force Command
—Arizona Sector . . . August 15, 1976—9:45 P.M.*

Brig. Gen. Oliver Quentin Hardyman poured himself a short bourbon over ice. It was his third in the past hour. His well-supplied command tent included a small refrigerator and he kept the ice compartment filled. Hardyman tested the drink and added a touch more bourbon. Slowly, his mind occupied, he returned to the littered field table that served as his desk. Three brown service records lay on top of the pile.

Hardyman sat down, leaned back in his chair, and stared at the three army service jackets. He had read and reread them. He now felt he knew enough of the situation to make a decision, even if he was unable to gather more information. He tried not to think about the three letters he had to write. There was a knock at the door frame of the general's tent.

"Enter." The general looked up from his desk absently.

"General." A short man in fresh army fatigues

stepped in and let the door close behind him. The informality of the two men made it plain that they were old friends.

"Major. Nice evening out?"

"Not bad, considering all the damn dust we've been kicking up all afternoon. Just sorta hangs in the air, ya know?"

"Get yourself a bourbon to wash out your tonsils and let's talk." As the major busied himself with ice and glass, the general picked up the top service jacket.

"After some consideration," he began as if talking to himself, "I think this man was the fly in the ointment."

"Sir?" The major turned, his drink only half mixed.

"I said, I believe Private Dickson may have been the cause of that fire fight."

"Dickson?"

"Yes, and if his company commander ever gets here we'll probably know for sure. Here, you take a look at this service record." The general handed the entire folder across the littered table to the major who took it and sat down opposite him. A short silence followed while the major skimmed the service record.

"It appears, General, you could be right. This kid was a troublemaker and it looks like he got what was coming to him."

"My opinion exactly, Fred. His father is no doubt just like him. Look at that security check. Of all the people to have on the front line! If the press ever got hold of that they'd have a field day! He's the only one of the three that failed to get clearance for that special project his unit was assigned to a year ago, mostly because of his father and partly because of those two arrests." The general lit a cigarette. "I'm sure as hell glad we didn't push on through that perimeter."

"You get the final report on that yet?"

"Yes. From what they were able to piece together out there, it's probable that at least one Indian was badly wounded, probably killed, judging from the amount of blood he lost. One horse dead. He was left where he fell. Dickson's automatic rifle clip was empty. The rifle was in the bunker and Dickson was quite a distance toward the Indian's known position." The general paused, sipped his drink, and reflected on what he'd just said. "We'll never know for sure, Fred, but I think Dickson may have just shot one of those outriders because he was red."

"It's a damn good thing you held up that attack order . . . " The major was still looking at the record in his lap. " . . . just a damn good thing."

"Enter." The general responded to a rap at the door. A young, sharply outfitted captain stepped in and came forward.

"Captain P.R. Ferguson reporting as ordered, General."

The general returned his salute.

"At ease, Captain."

"Thank you, sir."

"Captain," the major spoke up, "are you familiar with the service record of Phil Dickson?"

"Only vaguely, sir. I held command of my unit for only two weeks before we were called up."

"Did you know about his arrests?"

"No, sir, I wasn't aware of any arrests."

"That's too bad, Captain. You may have saved a couple of lives had you been. Here, take a look." The major handed the service record to the captain. "It appears from what we have learned the other two soldiers with him and possibly one or two Indians may have paid for Dickson's background."

The captain shook his head as he looked over the clearance form. "I'm sorry, General. I just wasn't given time . . . . "

"We're all sorry, Captain. Thank you, you're dismissed." A visibly shaken young captain saluted and left.

"Fred."

"Quint?"

"Tell our troops to hold at ready until I hear from Washington. I don't know how I'm going to explain. I'm not going to bet on a kid arrested for cross-burning whose old man is in the KKK. Hate is hate and I don't personally hate those Indians. But, once we start fighting them, we'll have to kill every last one before they'll quit. I don't want that on my conscience . . . not if I can avoid it."

"Nor I, Quint." The major set down his glass. "I'll see to it that the company commanders receive the new orders."

*United Nations, Security Council—New York City
...August 16, 1976—1:55 A.M.*

"Mr. Chairman . . . " The delegate of the United
States asked to be recognized and was.

"The United States of America wishes to express its
displeasure at the calling of an emergency session, and
the implication thereof. The matter upon which you
have been requested to act is an internal matter over
which the United Nations has no jurisdiction . . . . "

"Point of order, Mr. Chairman."

"The Chair recognizes India."

"Thank you, Mr. Chairman." The small man with
fine brown hands spoke softly. "May I remind the
United States that Anishinabe-waki has been recognized as a sovereign nation and is therefore entitled to
the protection of this body. Thank you, Mr. Chairman."

The Indian resumed his seat as the delegate of the
USSR signaled the podium. He began with sure au-
thority as though reading from a prepared text.

"Mr. Chairman, may I remind the honorable representative of the United States that he and his country, the United States of America, have used this forum countless times to chide other member nations about their treaty commitments. He may object to this meeting but he cannot deny fact.

"As a self-appointed watchdog, the United States has, at the slightest provocation, brought to the attention of this council of nations any and all variances or violations of treaty commitments. It has done so at the same time as it has encouraged such incidents behind the mask of world policeman which it has seen fit to don, without, I might add, the request of any other nation.

"Therefore, it only seems right and most appropriate to remind the United States of the four-hundred-odd treaties it has broken with the nations of our newest member, Anishinabe-waki and to mention that, without regard for the people of these nations, it has taken untold liberties with the monies, land, and even the children of these nations, using as its tool the omnipresent Bureau of Indian Affairs.

"Through manipulation of treaties, illegal transfer of land titles, threats, malpractice, and open oppression of the peoples within these nations, the United States has systematically and maliciously attempted to reduce the lands held by the nations of Anishinabe-waki to a faint and painful memory. Their methods have, in large measure, worked.

"Now they appear here at this world forum with

sullen faces, perhaps even a feigned repentance, at the same time as their troops mass along the borders of Anishinabe-waki in preparation to crush, once and for all, these troublesome nations who have managed to survive despite the worst possible odds.

"My government urges this council to use its strongest and most urgent methods to compel the United States of America to withdraw from the boundaries of the states of Anishinabe-waki and cease its aggression against this new nation.

"My people, the people of the Union of Soviet Socialist Republics, stand alongside the people of India, ready to come to the aid of Anishinabe-waki should it become necessary. Our aircraft are now delivering to the states of this new nation supplies of a peaceful nature. May I remind the United States that the accords of the Geneva Arab-Israeli pact of last year provide free access to any nation via assigned free international air space and that no act of aggression may be taken against such efforts.

"The United States should bear in mind that any attempt to halt efforts to aid our new member will be considered an act of aggression against the USSR, and will be answered with proper retaliation. The world is watching.

"We cannot allow this arrogant and hungry giant to crush under its iron fist this new nation. My people will not stand for it and we call on all people of conscience to rally to this cause. . . . I will close with a warning to the Canadian oppressor: this reminder serves for your actions as well. Thank you, Mr. Chairman."

The large room erupted into a riot of applause that continued unabated for nearly five minutes. A recess was called, emptying the room of all delegates except the honorable ambassador from the United States who sat glumly and silently, staring at the podium. At that moment he and ol' Charlie Graham had something in common. It was another one of those days.

Consulate of India—New York City . . .
August 16, 1976—3:59 A.M.

The two men were tired. Their faces showed the strain of long, sleepless hours spent dealing with new developments on what seemed to be an hourly basis. They sat quietly in a small drawing room, relaxing with freshly brewed tea. For a brief period, reports and paperwork were put aside for the simple pleasure of companionship.

"It has been a long day, a very long day." Roy Bear Walks Backward stretched his long arms, then relaxed and smiled slightly. "Tired, Krishna?"

"Yes, my good friend, I am most weary." Krishna Nadcarny smiled, his peaceful eyes still bright, though his body indeed felt the weight of his efforts.

"This has been an exciting couple of years for us, my friend, and it looks like it could start moving even faster, eh?"

"There is little doubt we are on a fast horse—perhaps one of your war ponies." A sip of tea returned the gentle smile to Krishna's face. He had warm feelings for the large man with fur-wrapped braids. "There has always been a kinship between our peoples in a distant fashion, Roy. Now we ride the same horse. I, for one, do not regret our decision to support your people two years ago, though I'm sure you could have found an ally with far superior resources."

"Perhaps in material ways. But we weren't really looking for that kind of support. The internal strength you have shown has meant far more than tanks or bombs, Krishna. As you said, our peoples know similar paths. We have each paid a dear price for what we hold close to our hearts."

Indeed, the kinship between the people of India and the native people of the Americas was greater than the superficial likeness of their names—the white man's designation born of a navigational blunder. Both nations were characterized by cultures within cultures, many racial types within one people, and by languages and dialects which differed completely within only a few miles of each other; and, of course, the main bond was that each had known at what cost freedom from oppression had to be bought. Each had suffered at the hands of the white man who brought his so-called civilization to the poor, backward natives, each had fought the white man, each had fought, bled, and died in an effort to remain free. The people of India had watched as their way of life perished amidst the relentless European passion to spread "civilization."

Roy lit a cigarette and wadded up the empty pack. He had also gained a fondness for tea through his association with his friend from so far away. They had spent many hours together working toward the alliance that had brought them to that point. It had not always been easy, but difficult times had bonded their friendship to last a lifetime. Roy's gaze came to rest on the gentle eyes of his friend.

"Krishna, if we get through this it is my hope to visit your homeland. Our peoples must come to know each other."

"It is my wish, also, Roy. There is much we have to share. Let us finish our tea and think on these things while we sleep. We will have much to do when the sun rises, my friend."

Roy lifted his cup to his brother.

"To the people of our homelands. May they share what they have together."

"The Creator's blessings on you, my friend."

Lakota . . . August 16, 1976—About noon

Al Lame Crow looked disgusted. "It's those damn BIA councilmen again, Joel. They say we can't hold them. They keep crying about 'rights.'"

"What rights? Until this is settled, they have no rights." Joel Turning Hawk spoke softly, but in a matter-of-fact tone. "They should have considered someone else's rights a long time ago. Now they'll have time to think on it." His hair hung loose about his shoulders, his face looked rested. "Whose *rights* did they consider in '73 when the Movement tried to claim its rights? Unfortunately for our fine Apples, the U.S. Indian-fighters can't get in this time to help them. The bastards! Let 'em stew."

Al grinned. "I'll give 'em the message."

Joel did not particularly care for the way the Movement had handled itself in 1973. He felt Wounded Knee had been a waste of lives, especially since the American people hadn't given a damn about a few dead Indians. The ideas behind the occupation had just seemed to drift over the heads of middle-class Americans and off to never-never land. The typical response to an unpleasant situation was: "If we don't look at it, it will go away." Besides, well-managed propaganda had caused the government to come out looking like a gentle, kind uncle, and the Movement a bunch of bums. They *had* been misguided in methods and scale perhaps, but they were hardly bums. Bums don't put their lives on the line for ideals; bums have no ideals. The men in the Movement had some very real ideals and two had died to prove it, only to be ignored by a complacent middle class of sheep who, if they gave any thought to Indians at all, still thought all Indians lived in teepees ... or should.

The idea of an Indian nation had not been born at Wounded Knee that long spring in 1973. The 1973 incident *had* made some people start thinking in the right direction. What appeared to the outside world was quite different from what actually went on. It was a sure bet the government had let out only what it wanted publicized and had stifled the rest. And the resulting trial of Indians was almost completely ignored by the media. The nation of Anishinabe-waki was not the result of public protest in the early part of the decade, but those actions had helped to spread the word. Unity among tribes was once unheard of; today it was a reality. Relations were touchy in some situations, but then Maine hardly ever agrees with Mississippi either. The United States are united when it's for the common good. It had taken time for the tribes to understand this, but it had come to pass and the Nishnabe were living proof. It would work, too, if fate gave it a chance.

Looking back, it was almost impossible to say just when Anishinabe-waki was born. Possibly, it was considered long before Joel Turning Hawk's grandfather was born. The idea of some sort of Indian unity was at least four hundred years old. Joel himself couldn't pinpoint when he had become an active part of it. He felt he had always been moving toward this end. He had participated in his first Sun Dance at the age of fourteen. Now, at twenty-seven, he had been pierced five times. Anishinabe-waki was as much a part of him as he was of it. It wasn't just the Sioux Nation; it was Nishnabe . . . the People!

The labor pains were not new. In a way, they had been harder to bear before, because it had been necessary to keep the fact that a birth was expected from the prying eyes of the government. Now the labor was in full force and the screams could be uttered out loud.

Few people knew better than Indians how to withstand pain. From the crushing defeat in King Philip's War in 1676 to the slaughter at Wounded Knee in 1890, the Indian people had had plenty of practice hiding their pain. The wounds ran deep. But the long, quiet memory of the red man had kept faith in his people and now, perhaps, the wounds would start to heal. With nations, as with all things, new birth brings hope.

The leaders of this new nation were as varied as the

one hundred fifty separate languages and dialects spoken by its people. From the young war chief of the Lakota to the members of the Executive Council, each man offered his own unique gift to the leadership of the Nishnabe. They had worked in secret with little support for a long time, but early in the decade that support began to grow. The young ones such as Joel became the legs and eyes of the elders. While the latter absorbed information, the former developed plans based on that information, gathering men and materials for the final effort. What began as a miniscule scattering of men grew into a silent army. Perhaps it was all the more easy to act without fear of detection because the United States chose to ignore its longest-standing citizens.

The reservations, once hated and scorned as ghettos without buildings, now offered a land base, a ready-made country. The territory was outlined and occupied; only the borders needed to be secured and that had been accomplished within the first forty-eight hours. Once this was done, the legality of the effort was put before the world forum, the United Nations. The next step, undisputed independence, would not be easy but the Nishnabe were prepared to wait it out. Now, with new supplies pouring in from throughout the world by way of Ghana, which had become a central distribution point, the Nishnabe could wait as long as necessary. Each day that the United States and Canada were held off gave them more time to grow from within. The pressure was now on the major powers—the Nishnabe cause had become a factor in the delicate balance of power. The chance that a full-scale military offensive would be mounted against the new nation decreased with each passing day. Supplies flowed in while the fabric which holds a people together grew stronger. Time was on the side of the Nishnabe.

"Joel...." A voice brought the young war chief's thoughts back to the present.

Walter Standing Elk stood in the doorway of the small office that was now Turning Hawk's base of operations.

"Yes, Walt?"

"The N.G. sergeant is here to see you. You know . . . the one who brought over those civilians and equipment."

A smile crossed Joel's dark features. "Oh yeah. Send him in. Been wanting to speak to him . . . . Wallace Youngblood, isn't it?"

"That's right. English name or Indian? He says Indian, but he sure doesn't look it . . . at least not Sioux."

"Now what the hell kinda remark is that? Don't look Indian!" Wallace Youngblood pushed his way past a startled Standing Elk. "What the hell does an Indian look like? You?" Youngblood jabbed a stubby finger, first at Standing Elk, then over to Joel's direction. "Or Turning Hawk here? Just what the fuck am I supposed to look like? You sound like some goddamn anthro. Shit! That's one hell of a remark coming from

an Indian. I think you've seen too many fuck'n movies
. . . . Looks like an Indian, my ass! Would you be
happy if I looked like Jeff Chandler?"

"Christ, don't get warped outta shape, Sarge! Didn't
mean . . . . " Walt Standing Elk looked sheepish.
"Guess that was kinda dumb, huh?"

"Real white of you, I'd say." Joel stood and reached
across the desk to shake hands with the former guardsman.

"Been looking forward to seeing you, Wallace.
Quite a stunt you pulled. Any more tricks up your
sleeve? Might need 'em if the U.S. doesn't start playing by the rules. They're getting pushy in the Southwest."

They touched hands lightly as was Indian custom,
so different from the white man's way which always
seems like a contest to see who can break whose hand
first.

"Nice to meet the war chief I've heard so much
about since I got over here." Wallace smiled. "You've
made quite a name for yourself, Chief."

Joel returned the smile. "Well, I've had one hell of
a lot of help." He motioned Youngblood to a chair and
sat back down himself. "Just outta curiosity . . . is
Youngblood English?"

"Honestly don't know. I do know I'm one-quarter
Sac-Fox and that makes me as much a part of this as
you are. As a matter of fact, those white boys who
came over with me are also Nishnabe as far as I'm
concerned. You know as well as I do that it's a feeling,

not a bloodline! Your former BIA-approved chief is proof of that! Full-blood, my ass! That fuck'n idiot! Let's face it, some of us have just paled out a little. Granddaddy just liked white girls."

"Well . . . that bloodline business is a bad habit we picked up from whites. They got to have a name and class for everybody, and once stuck, it's hard to shake loose. But Nishnabe is a state of mind, as you said, and I believe with time it will no longer matter about bloodlines. It's not the true way of our forefathers and it's long past time we corrected it. But I guess for many it'll take time."

"Can't blame some of the older folks. That's about all the identity the whites left 'em. Now, or at least in the near future, a lot of that will change."

"Well, Nishnabe is an identity." Joel asked Walt to see if they could get some coffee sent in. After he was gone, Turning Hawk lowered his voice a bit. "Look, Sarge, don't hold that remark against Walt. I'm sure he just was reacting outta habit."

"Oh, shit . . . I know that! Just sorta gets old after a while. I don't hold no grudges, though. I'll speak to him later. Kinda like the guy anyway."

"He's all right, believe me. Now I'd like to talk some about your little group."

"Shoot." Youngblood settled back. Walt returned with three cups of coffee and settled himself on the table, cross-legged.

"Shoot what?" he said blowing on the steaming cup of black liquid.

"We're just about to get into what we're gonna do with Sergeant Youngblood's little troop." Joel grinned. "Isn't every day someone brings us three tanks, along with the people to run them!"

"Well . . ." Walt set down his cup. "They've all gone through the IPF boys and, except for the UN guy, they got clean bills. Matter of fact, four more claim to be Indian. Seems to me that N.G. unit had better start checking its people a little closer. Looks like half of their entire unit is Indian. Course they wouldn't know an Indian from a football," he grinned at Youngblood, "but we do, huh, Sarge?"

"Some of us, anyway." Youngblood couldn't help laughing. The three men understood this was Walt's way of saying he'd been wrong. It wouldn't be mentioned again.

"Wallace, do you have any doubts that your boys will fight for us?" Joel was dead serious now.

"Frankly, no. They will or they wouldn't be here. They know the odds on all-out assault by the U.S. It would seem most of these guys are tired of being used by the high mucky-mucks as pawns in their war games. The president picks a spot and declares a private war, then—zap! You're off to get killed for his personal pleasure. The president is going to have some trouble keeping Indian-fighters. The morale is rotten!"

"Perhaps," Joel let a slight grin flicker across his features, "just perhaps, the U.S. has forgotten what men will die for. A country . . . a flag . . . an idea . . .

but I seriously doubt they care to die for a president, a man they have lost respect for. They probably realize we're no threat to their national security—just to the president's big party plans."

"That's right," Standing Elk chimed in. "We've only held what is ours, except for a few towns built on our land anyway. We can't take back the whole damn country, and we don't want to. Just want to keep what is left to us. Look at the mess those whites have made of the rest of it!"

"Yeah." Youngblood looked troubled. "At the rate the BIA was selling off our land, it wouldn't last another ten years."

Joel laughed. "After all, our people have only been here sixty thousand years. If we like it, we just might decide to stay!"

Youngblood grinned. "Yeah, but Joel, ya know just by looking at me that I'm not a traditionalist like you. First, I don't believe that all white culture is bad. Second, I'm just not ready to go back to the 'old way,' at least not completely. I hope you understand what I'm trying to say."

Joel leaned back in his chair. "I think so, but go on."

"O.K." Wallace squared his shoulders. "You know yourself that we've had an alien culture forced on us —they call it 'freedom.' To me freedom is the choice one makes for himself. I'm not about to forget I'm Nishnabe but I know where I draw the line for myself. We need to be free to choose our own path as long as we hurt no one in the process." Wallace leaned forward. "That's why those white boys are here. The Establishment has gotten so hung up on the idea of freedom that the white man has forgotten what it looks like. I pray to God that we never do. Not all whites are bad, and you know damn good and well that all Indians aren't sweethearts, right?"

"Right, Sergeant. I don't agree with you on all the details, but I agree in principle. I pray also. The words are probably different but it's for the same understanding. I don't hate the white man; I hate the idea of 'white.' It's not a culture but a machine of destruction. It destroys a man on the inside and leaves an empty shell. I understand how you feel. If I didn't, I don't think we'd be any better off now than before. If we don't profit from the mistakes the white man has made, then we are bigger fools than he is."

Youngblood nodded. His countryman continued. "Yes, Wallace. For myself, the old way is best, but I wouldn't ask you to go that far if you don't feel it. That, my friend, is what this whole thing is all about."

Standing Elk crossed his legs on the table and finished off his coffee.

"This stuff, I love—coffee—*pejuta-sapa* we call it. Something the white man brought to the Lakota. Sorta like taking the chaff from the grain. I ain't no statesman but I know one thing: You don't throw the baby out with the bath water!" Youngblood laughed.

"Right on, brother! Which reminds me, just how are you running this show?"

"Very simple." Joel declined the cigarette Youngblood offered. "Each state has a chairman and council. The Mohawks have also kept their clan system—after all, it's worked well for a few thousand years. Anyway, the chairman and council are under the Executive Council which is made up of seven men from all three states. For now, that's it. Until this war is over the Executive Council will act for all of us on the international level."

"Sounds all right." Youngblood lit his cigarette. "Now where do you want my boys and the tanks?"

Bethesda, Maryland . . . August 17, 1976—Evening

Ed Small Wolf sat, drink in hand, letting his mind wander over the events of the last few weeks. The fact that his movements were controlled by the agents assigned to him for the duration had become a part of daily life. After the first few days both he and Susan had come to accept the role they expected to play out as long as the war lasted. Ed had, with the assistance of his friend Col. Harold Jackson, been granted certain "freedoms." After the UN intervened, he was allowed limited contact with the Anishinabe-waki Executive Council.

At first the council wanted no part of him, but after learning of his feelings and his present position they changed their attitude. They realized that his talents would be useful to their new nation once hostilities ceased and, since he no longer considered himself a member of the United States Congress, throwing away those talents would serve the interest of no one.

Roy Bear Walks Backward, head of the council,

knew how hard Ed had worked to get to Congress. He had started out like most Pine Ridge boys, growing up under the ever-present weight of hunger and cold which were part of life for most poorer Sioux living on the reservation. His family had a two-room cabin, completely lacking in modern conveniences: no water, no lights, no indoor plumbing—in fact, no floor. Despite the living conditions and the sad excuse for a school he attended, he managed to become a first-rate student. His three brothers were smart but lacked Ed's drive. For him, school became the way out. By the time he reached the age of seventeen, he knew what he wanted and which way to go to get it. The Sioux needed lawyers, he felt, and come hell or high water, he was going to be one.

He had met Susan Zimmerman when he was a junior in high school. Despite her name, she was a full-blood Sioux and the daughter of one of the men who had managed to climb out of the reservation's poverty to gain a good education. Susan's father took a special interest in Ed, and through his assistance the young man found his way through the BIA paper mill and red tape, ending up at Harvard Law School. He gained his law degree and his wife about the same time, both of which pleased Susan's father.

From there to Congress, Ed never stopped working for his people. Unfortunately, his position had put a wall between him and those for whom he was working so hard. It grew slowly and quietly, going completely unnoticed by Ed or Susan, until the Lakota had taken to the warpath. Only then did Ed realize how far he had drifted away from his people. The weeks since that realization had been full of painful soul-searching and a total reevaluation of what he was and what road he would follow from there. At thirty-three he was forced back to "go."

It was really a process of finding out what he wasn't. Once he determined that, he had a starting point. Somehow, the point at which he found himself was also the point at which he had lost himself five years before. Now he had to rebuild his life. Difficult as he and Susan knew it would be, he hated just sitting, waiting, marking time until Anishinabe-waki won its independence. But there was little he could do beyond waiting. And he was certain that it would come to pass.

"Honey." Susan's voice broke through the haze. She was standing barefoot in the doorway of the kitchen. "Honey, are you hungry?"

"Not really, but if I don't mix something with this booze, I'm going to end up drunk as a jaybird. What's to eat?" Before Susan could answer, the doorbell rang.

"Oh, shit! Big Brother again!" Ed headed for the door. "Second thought, fix me another drink." Ed opened the door to see Hal Jackson looking grim. "Make that two drinks," he called to Susan over his shoulder.

"Mind if I drink it inside?" Hal was still standing on the small porch in the hot evening air. Ed grinned.

"Just to show you how fair a fellow I am, you can

even sit down." He motioned Hal in, thumbed his nose at the agents watching from their car at the curb, and shut the door. After weeks of this routine, there had developed a playful attitude between the Small Wolfs and the agents assigned to them. He got the door shut before the man behind the wheel could return the compliment.

"One point for our side!" Ed called out to Susan.

Susan floated into the room, drinks in hand. "For you, Big Brother." She handed Hal his and, in one motion, handed Ed his and gave him a loving peck on the cheek. "You're off and running, huh, jaybird?" She left the room, propelled by a firm smack on her bottom.

"I'm glad you're in a good mood." Hal took a long pull on his drink. "The president wants to talk to you."

Ed's smile disappeared. "Now what the hell for?" He called to his wife. "Susan, you'd better hear this."

"Well," Hal stalled, "actually, I haven't any idea. General Sherman sent me over here to get you and that's all I know about it."

"Ah, come on, Hal, you've got to have some idea what's on his mind." Jackson felt a bit uncomfortable with both Susan, who was sitting on the arm of Ed's chair, and the tall Indian looking at him. Their look was like a shower of darts pinning him to his chair.

"All right. If Sue will fix me another drink, I'll tell you what I know. But I warn you . . . it isn't much, not much at all." He drained his glass.

Oval Office of the President—Washington, D.C.
. . . August 17, 1976—9:00 P.M.

The news media had been running wild since Ani-shinabe-waki had launched her first sortie back in July. It was Christmas every day, always something new and always something to make bold headlines of. The press changed positions quickly, from pro to con, depending on who got in the best licks on any particular day. Like a fickle woman, it would attack the president one morning only to support his position, such as it was, that evening. Since there had been little in the way of blood and guts in the war, the newsmen contented themselves with making even the most boring development appear like a landmark. In all fairness, they had made a lot of dull maneuvering seem quite interesting. Without their efforts, it would have been the most do-nothing war in history. In fact, they were not above trying to push one side or the other into doing something that would make good copy. The fire fight at Cabolclo had been made to look like another Pork Chop Hill. To the surprise of no one, it had also been compared to the defeat of one general who put his foot in it up to his knee on the Little Big Horn River one hot June day a hundred years before.

The president, being a very press-conscious person, insisted on keeping up with this torrent of news, which didn't help his headaches in the least. It was, in fact, an article in the Washington *Post* which referred to Congressman Edward Small Wolf as a political prisoner that prodded him into calling Ed to his private quarters that hot, muggy evening. Something had to be done about this man. What that something was had not yet come to him when Ed arrived with Colonel Jackson and two agents in tow.

"Good evening, Congressman," the president said, his voice tinged with ice.

"Mr. President," Ed nodded. "If you'll excuse me, sir, it's Mister. I'm no longer a congressman."

"Once a congressman, always a congressman, I think you'll find . . . er . . . Mr. Small Wolf." The president was plainly strained. "Now Mr. Small Wolf, did you give out this nonsense about being a political prisoner?"

Ed smiled but didn't answer.

"Well, Mr. Small Wolf?"

"Mr. President, you know as much about what I've done as I do. My every move has been recorded or reported to you." Ed's smile was gone. "My only contact with my people had been through your own representatives. My statements were not direct, but relayed, I'm sure, via your office. The answer to your question is a definite no. Not that I don't agree with the statement; I've just had no chance to say it myself."

"Your people have had the opportunity."

"I wouldn't know, Mr. President. I suggest you check your own house if you doubt what I've said."

"What, sir, are you suggesting?"

"Only that there may well be rough edges, Mr. President. You've been a politician longer than I."

Though the president continued to hold his steely gaze into the calm, dark eyes of Small Wolf, he directed his next statement to Jackson.

"Colonel, this envelope contains orders for you to arrange priority transportation for Mr. Small Wolf and his wife to the consulate of India in New York." He handed Jackson the envelope and fixed his eyes once again on the Indian. "Now, sir, whatever the reason behind this story, it has lost its basis. Goodnight, Mr. Small Wolf."

The president watched the door shut, wondering if he had indeed silenced the rumor mill. The idea that his own house might not be in order was hardly new to him.

Bethesda, Maryland ... August 17, 1976—11:15 P.M.

As Ed opened the door, the living room was filled with the high-pitched war chant of the Northern Plains. Thunder drums vibrated, setting the walls athrob with the beat of knowing hands. Susan sat in a large chair, her arms around her knees and eyes closed, swaying gently to the ancient rhythm. She didn't even hear him come in. She was lost in some memory of days at home, nights under the stars, of family, of her people.

Ed smiled as he slowly turned down the stereo, watching her pretty face. Her dark eyes opened and she returned the smile.

"Big White Chief speak plenty?" she asked, grinning.

Ed crossed the room in easy strides and picked her up in his arms, gently kissing her soft, brown face.

"Pack, Squaw. Big White Chief say: get on your pony and ride. Honey, we're going home!"

Her eyes widened. "You mean Dakota?"

"Lakota now, and yes we're going home, via New York."

"A little out of the way, isn't it?" She was beaming anyway.

"Let's get started with the packing and I'll explain. We don't have much time so I'm afraid we'll have to leave a lot behind. Take only what we really need. Maybe we'll get the rest later, but you should know that it isn't likely." He had dreaded telling her that part of it.

Her eyes laughed. "I don't care.... Let's just go home!" And he swung her around the room, the tribal music still covering them with the beat of the thunder drum.

"Well, tell me, tell me. We've got work to do." She was headed for the bedroom to start breaking camp. "Why New York and how did we get outta prison?"

"It seems Mr. President got the idea that I put out the story about being a political prisoner. Naturally, I explained that wasn't likely since I hadn't talked to anyone other than his people. Don't really think he believed me. Doesn't trust his own people, I guess." Ed was busy taking down suitcases from the closet when the doorbell rang.

"Well, damn . . . eleven-thirty at night and they still bug us."

His surprise was ill-concealed as he opened the

door. Keller Dillman, senior senator from Maine, stood smiling on the small porch.

"Senator Dillman? Aren't you out consorting with the enemy a little late?" Ed invited him in. He turned the stereo off.

"Well, Congressman, it's trying to decide who the enemy is that has me out this late. Got a drink around?" Senator Dillman was known for his large capacity for liquor and made no effort to hide it. His florid complexion belied the keen mind and ready wit of an experienced and very capable administrator, top politician, and long-time Senate watchdog. It appeared he had picked up a scent and was on the trail again. "My sources tell me you were being sprung and I'm just here to say good luck."

"No offense intended, Senator, but I see the fin of a shark." He handed the senator his drink. "Couldn't be that you smell blood?"

"Whose? Yours, mine, or somebody else's?" Dillman was enjoying the scotch.

"Well, as for me, I'm not bleeding . . . at least not so I've noticed it anyway. How about some straight talk . . . or just a nice drink. Either one will do but I'm not going to fence with an old pro like you. After all you're not known to be pro-Indian."

"I'm not known to be anti-Indian either." Dillman smiled. "I won't pretend that I approve of what your people have done but it's what made them do it that concerns me. As you and I both know, our president relies very little on the old advise and consent concept.

Where Anishinabe-waki is concerned, he has the power to crush your movement without even consulting the House or Senate. I want to be sure that he doesn't crush humans in the process. That would deal us a mortal internal wound from which we could not recover."

"Do you think he will crush us?" Ed's face gave no indication of emotion.

"Son, I think he'd crush his mother if she crossed him up." Dillman held out an empty glass and Ed refilled it. "Our president may not be the most intelligent man to ever hold that office, but he's not a fool either. He will wait, and when he has an opening, he'll slash your throats with all the finesse of a Samurai—quick, clean, and easy. Believe me, son, he can do it and I think he'll try." Dillman tested his drink and put on his smile again. "My only concern is that if he does, he doesn't lop off more than he intends. He's made one big mistake in abolishing the BIA. Right now he could sure use the help of the Indians in the bureau, but no; he over-reacted and cut off his nose to spite his face. 'Friendlies,' as the army calls them, could provide him with some insight, which at the present moment he is in desperate need of to avoid a very costly blunder. Not that it would be new to him. Hell, man, you don't have all the Indians in the U.S. on your side."

Ed didn't try to deny that fact.

"Not by a long shot . . . ." Dillman sunk deeper in his chair. "I'm one-sixteenth Pennobscot, and I'm not joining Anishinabe-waki. I don't need to tell you that according to our laws, that makes me an Indian too. Just about like half the goddamn population of the U.S. for that matter! Unfortunately, our president isn't concerned with what that population may want. His only concern is that he may lose some of what other administrations have managed to steal." Ed smiled.

"That's right," Dillman nodded. "I don't deny Indians have been screwed, but it's still the country I'm concerned with—not just Indians or this administration's record."

"Frankly, Senator, I'm not concerned with the country *or* the administration—only Indians."

"You'd better be, son. Even if you are Nishnabe, Anishinabe-waki sits right in the middle of this country and if the U.S. goes, what makes you think you won't too?" He held up an empty glass. "It's like Canada says, 'It's a little like sleeping with an elephant,' and that's why I'm here, Small Wolf. If the United States hiccups you'll feel the shock wave clear up your spine."

"I'm making you no promises, Senator," Ed said as he handed Dillman his refill, "so expect none."

"That's not what I want. Just promise yourself something."

"What?"

"My information tells me you're to meet with the Nishnabe Executive Council, right?" Susan came into the room. The senator nodded and went right on. "If that's the case, you can help your people and mine. We don't need any more boys killed on either side, but it's going to take some effort to keep the president from using force on Anishinabe-waki if he gets the chance. He's already mobilizing transport jets to pull troops back from Europe and that means only one thing: He wants to stop you cold."

Ed frowned. "Even with Russia and India in the middle?"

"I'm telling you, son, he'll do it with Congress in the middle, if he can, and the U.S. can't afford it." Dillman sat forward. "We can't afford to cut up our own insides. There are enough people trying to do it for us." Dillman relaxed again. "I don't think independence is the answer for Anishinabe-waki, but I'm not ready to bomb them out of existence either."

"Senator, just how much did you have to do with my being let out of this little prison?"

"Enough to get the job done."

"The fin breaks water." Ed laughed. "I knew none of my people planted that story. Now you expect me to act as a buffer, a go-between?"

Dillman shifted his hulking body. "I don't put your talents as low on the scale as you do. I think you can act on your own once you get out of here. I am simply trying to tell you that care must be taken to preserve both our unions. The world is watching, son, and the buzzards are poised to pick all our bones clean. Perhaps the Nishnabe can find their independence, but— and I warn you—it can't be at the expense of killing the U.S. You would be cutting your own throat."

"Senator, I am smart enough to see the wisdom in what you say. However, I'm not on the Executive Council." Ed drained his glass and asked Susan to refill it. She had sat quietly on the arm of his chair and just as quietly went to fix him another drink. "I'll make no promises, but I'll consider all this very carefully. My actions with the council will take this conversation into account."

Susan returned and handed Ed his drink. She broke her silence.

"Senator Dillman, do you want to see us crushed?"

"Mrs. Small Wolf, I simply don't want to see our union die because some oversized ego can't let a new nation breathe. I do not see Anishinabe-waki as a threat . . . . Change, yes; threat, no. If we can exist together, then we shall do so . . . if we are allowed to."

Two hours later, the Small Wolfs were on a special flight from Andrews Air Force Base on their way to New York and the consulate of India.

*Somewhere on the High Plains—
Land of the Lakota Nation . . . Circa 1870*

*Foam from the running pony's mouth splattered back on
bare legs, making the red war paint run in the wind. The
red-streaked thighs of the warrior strained as they gripped the
horse's heaving sides. At a dead run, he approached the orderly
line of dismounted troops. A clipped yelp followed by the long,
drawn-out scream of Dog Soldier's war cry burst from his dry
lips.*

*At twenty-five yards, pressure from his knees turned the
"paint" at a right angle to the soldiers as he loosed the first
arrow from his bow. A trooper gripped the quivering shaft
as it protruded from his chest and sprawled forward on the
dry brown grass. The warrior let go his second arrow before
the soldier's body had hit the ground; another blue-coat felt
the metal-pointed shaft.*

*Then, as the third arrow left his bow, the gleaming row
of Springfields belched smoke. A rain of bullets fell on horse
and rider, the sickening thud of lead on flesh echoed the
roar of rifles. A piercing scream left the throat of the war pony
as his front legs buckled. The warrior glimpsed blue sky and*

brown earth as if they had become one. His torn body threw up billows of dust as it met the ground in a deafening crush of human and animal. He was dead before he stopped rolling . . . .

Ed's eyes snapped open. His body was drenched. He assured himself it was sweat, not blood, trickling down his side and tried to get his bearings. He was in a room . . . the roar of rifles still rang in his ears but it was a pillow he clutched in his trembling hands. His mouth was dry and he was sure he could taste dust. Slowly regaining his self-control, he relaxed his grip on the pillow and turned his head to see Susan's pretty face, her hand on his shoulder.

"Ed, honey, you O.K.?" Her long black hair glistened in the half-light of the room. "Ed, are you all right?"

He was slow to answer; the words got caught in his dry throat. "Guess I just had a bad dream," he said trying to smile. He wanted to banish the fear in her eyes. " . . . Just a bad dream, honey. Sorry I woke you up."

He reached for the water glass on the nightstand, still not completely free of the picture of that line of blue-coats. His hand was unsteady as he washed the taste of dust from his mouth.

"Must have been some dream," Susan smiled. The fear gone, she lay back on her pillow. "Sound effects and all. Didn't know you could holler like that!"

"Neither did I." He drained the glass. "Actually hollered, huh?"

"Hollered? Hon, you screamed!" She giggled. "War whoop, you might call it."

"Yeah, you could call it that." He didn't elaborate. Man! It had been too real. He closed his eyes and, in an instant replay, he could still see it all: the line of troops, the dead war pony, and the broken body of the young warrior, twisted in death as if crumpled by a giant hand. Slowly the picture faded into blackness, his body relaxing a little and the sweat drying from his forehead. He listened till Susan's breathing told him she had gone back to sleep. She had been so tired when they arrived at the consulate he felt guilty about waking her, perhaps a little ashamed that he was showing the strain in front of her. But then, she had always shared his life completely, making his problems hers and never shirking her position when the going got rough; and it hadn't been easy these past couple of months. She hadn't complained, but when Roy Bear Walks Backward had greeted them on their arrival at the Indian consulate, she had cried a little. It was almost like coming home.

The big man had hugged them, spoken of happier times, then saw to it they were made comfortable. He had fussed over them like a father until he was sure the exhausted young couple was settled in.

Giving strict orders that they were to be left to rest completely, he had returned to the nonstop flow of work he and the council were facing. Lying on his back, Ed felt himself give in to the exhaustion he had held off so long. Susan's quiet, easy breathing, the cooling effect of the perspiration now drying off his body gave him a feeling of comfort. His racing mind slowed as sleep overcame him and, visions of bluecoats forgotten, he drifted off.

St. Lawrence River, near Quebec...
August 17, 1976—Dusk

The group stood next to the river bank. Darkness was coming in fast. The four Mohawks and seven white men had been talking for thirty minutes. Only one Mohawk had spoken; the rest stood silently near the two canoes on the shore.

A white man spoke. "Look, we need the alliance. We need your help, but these are important men."

"What do we look like? Rocks?" The Mohawk wasn't smiling.

"I didn't mean that, damn it! But you want us to send one of our top men and a French ambassador up river in boats to meet with your chiefs!"

"You asked to meet."

"Not like this!"

"You asked."

"Look, what about the patrols? What about all the places we could be spotted?"

"We won't be seen," the Mohawk grinned, "at least not as men."

"Now, what the hell does that mean?"

"We have strong medicine which will confuse the eyes of the enemy. We will appear as logs."

"Oh, for Christ's sake! You Indians haven't changed in two hundred years!"

"Perhaps you whites haven't learned in two hundred years." The Mohawk grinned again. "We got here, didn't we?"

Since the answer was apparent, the white man sputtered, "O.K., O.K., but look at your group! How long have you people been shaving your heads?"

"Do you mean our scalp locks?" All four Mohawks had traditional haircuts.

"Yeah, scalp locks, if that's what you call 'em."

"As long as you white men have been wearing shoes, maybe longer. Do your shoes affect the way you think or perform in a given situation?"

"Oh shit! Just a minute."

The white man held a short discussion with his group. He seemed to be protesting but was losing the battle. A man dressed in woodsman's clothes stepped forward.

"Brother, do you think we can get back to your area?"

"If I didn't think so, I would not try," said the Mohawk flatly.

"How long will it take?"

"Three or four nights. We do not press our medicine in daylight. We aren't fools."

"*C'est la guerre!* Let us be off!" Within minutes the

group was moving upriver toward Akwesasne: four Mohawks, a general in the Free French Forces, and a French ambassador with a great deal of bargaining power. In the daytime, the group rested, hiding in small inlets on the river or pulling the light canoes up on the bank, out of sight.

As they neared Akwesasne on the fourth night, the leader spoke softly. The two boats moved side by side and the white men were told to lie as low as possible. In the distance, the approach of a patrol boat could be heard.

"No noise." The leader of the Mohawk group said something to his men in their language. Then, with one hand over his mouth, he made the sound of a nighthawk. Once, twice, three times; then quiet. As the boat passed, voices carried over the water. Some conversation could be distinguished, especially the part about what would make logs float upriver. The medicine of the Mohawks was good.

A new treaty was in the making.

Oval Office of the President—Washington, D.C.
. . . August 18, 1976—6:55 A.M.

Reports from all fronts, including the UN, had been condensed and organized for the president. All did not appear well. The picture, in fact, was very grim. For the president this was to have been a big month in the bicentennial celebration. It was now turning into a nightmare. His headache had become a constant companion and the coffee didn't taste right.

"About all that's missing is our surrender." His words were directed to no one in particular. "Wonder when we'll get around to that?" He shuffled his papers.

"Mr. President." General Sherman looked beat. "We can crush this whole thing right now if you'll just give the order. Those Indians don't have a chance and you know it!"

"General, had you said that some months ago, I would have agreed with you, but not now . . . not now. This is not just one group of Indians in a little town in South Dakota!"

"Mr. President, I beg your pardon! We can blow them all to hell in fifteen minutes."

"General, I'm aware of our fire power! I'm also aware that at this time there are Russians, Indians, and God knows who else within Indian-held territory. Bombs know no favorites. We'll blow up the Indians, and we'll also blow up those other damn Indians along with some Russians.... Do you understand that we can't afford that? We, sir, are in check. For the moment, I'd say it could be checkmate."

"Mr. President." A square-faced man with curly hair and smallish features spoke.

"Yes, Mr. Schliger?"

"Sir, perhaps if you meet with them. Not on their territory . . . er, ours . . . er . . . well here, sir."

"Well, I'm sure as hell not going there! All they have are tom-toms, and 'Hail to the Chief' sounds like hell on drums. Besides, no president has ever stooped to going *to* the Indians! *They* come to the president!"

"But they have their own country now . . . . " Schliger knew he shouldn't have said that.

"Thanks, Harry. It seems I've heard rumors to that effect!" He poured himself another cup of coffee. "Damn!" he mumbled under his breath as he added Irish whiskey to the black brew. "Screw it," he thought to himself, and added an extra shot.

"General."

"Sir?"

"Do those Sioux know anything about the missiles they have?"

"We didn't think they did in the beginning, but then they've had over two months to rework them. I understand they have personnel that could do it. Especially since those Russians are making flights for 'peace' in there. A few pros and . . . "

"All right . . . that's what I was afraid of." The president rubbed a hand across his face. "Gentlemen, it may very well be checkmate."

Vice-President Browning had been sitting quietly. He now shifted his weight. "Mr. President, you're not really considering letting them win?"

"Letting them?" The president choked on a gulp of coffee. "Letting them!"

"Well, sir, that's what it sounds like."

"All right, Mr. Vice-President, perhaps you'd like to change hats before the election . . . if we have one."

"No, sir, I didn't mean that but . . . "

"But hell! Mind your own butt! We've been put against the wall and now it's panic time! We may not let them win but we have the small problem at this point of how not to lose! Are you all so stupid you can't see the spot we're in?"

He was answered with a deep, murky silence.

"Don't everyone speak at once!" The president folded his hands across his stomach and leaned back.

"All right, gentlemen, I have no desire to let our apparent ineptitude continue to grow while we slowly sink up to our ass in this mess." His eyes showed the spark of a warlord, his features were set in determination. "I am the president . . . not a military expert but, damn it to hell, as commander in chief, I have to act since my generals and advisors can't do their thing.

"At this point I can see no indication that letting the situation stand any longer is going to improve our position. We are losing ground but I do not intend to blow my head off like the late prime minister of Canada . . . though it might please more than a few.

"While we must appear to hold our positions, as stipulated by the UN, I want every possible pressure placed on the new allies of Anishinabe-waki. These so-called peace flights into their areas are carrying more than just peace. If we continue to wait, we'll have more Chinks and Russians in those areas than Indians. It will, I feel certain, reach the point where we can't let it continue, despite the cost!

"First we will twist a few international arms. If that fails . . . " The president leaned forward and fingered a letter opener. " . . . if that fails, gentlemen, we shall loose the hounds. You shall now prepare for that course of action. Need I say more?"

Gen. Tucker Sherman smiled.

Lakota . . . August 27, 1976—Late evening

The decided build-up of U.S. forces near the bound-aries of all three Nishnabe states had caused concern in the United Nations. The United States appeared to have decided to ignore the dictums of the world body and to act, instead, as it saw fit. These things weighed heavily on the mind of the young war chief of the Lakota.

Joel Turning Hawk rubbed his tired eyes. His du-ties had drawn on his strength and, though he ac-cepted his lot, it was not easy for him to spend hours reading reports and poring over data which now came in a torrent from the council. Reading was more the way of his cousin.

Thoughts of his cousin came to him as he leaned back in his chair. He was proud of Ed Small Wolf. He loved the man. In younger days, they had been close and, despite the age difference, they had been like brothers before Ed had gone away to the white man's school. Now both were again in the cause of which they had so often talked. Though Ed had gone from the home of his people, he had also followed the old way in younger years. He now wore a white shirt and tie, but beneath lay the scars of the Sun Dance.

Joel let his mind wander over these things and the events of the past few days: the reports of the Mohawk meeting with separatists and French in Quebec, the long deliberations with Eurasian powers which would help the Nishnabe. The talks had been good, the signs had been good. The news, which would shake Canada and Washington, would break soon.

In fact, the Nishnabe had signed pacts with two countries, an action that brought with it alignment with several others. They had, however, rejected the suggestion that they use the powerful Minutemen now in their possession against Washington. Certain world powers had tried to persuade the Lakota to do so but, unlike those powers, the Nishnabe were not dealers in death. To fight men is one thing; to destroy for the sake of destruction is another. It was not the way of the People.

The hour was late. Joel dozed, then half awoke when he felt someone near. He opened his eyes.

"My Chief." A light-skinned young man stood before him. His eyes were gray and his shoulder-length hair was brown.

"What is it?"

"My Chief, I have come from my quest. I have words for you."

"Are you Lakota? I do not know your face though you appear as they say our Strange One did."

"No, my Chief, though I do know of Crazy Horse. I am Shawnee."

"Your name?"

"I am called Maka Meen-de-gah."

"Your words?"

The young man was weak. He had not eaten in three days and he wavered a bit as he stood before Turning Hawk.

"It was on the third day. At the setting sun a tall man approached. He walked softly and on his right shoulder sat a beautiful hawk. He spoke after long moments of silence."

"Do you wish water, Maka Meen-de-gah?"

"Not until I have spoken."

"Then tell me, my brother."

"First he spoke of my medicine. He then told me to come to you. He said he had seen the People. They were many . . . as many as before. They would follow and soon to this land would come peace. We would be as we were. We would be the *People*. These are his words, my Chief. He left me then."

Joel spoke in a soft voice. "Rest now, my brother."

After the young man had left, Joel stripped. He put on a loin cloth and streaked yellow paint across his face. He then walked away to be alone and pray and wait for the rising sun. It was good.

Akwesasne . . . August 28, 1976—Afternoon

The area on the northern side of the border had been relatively quiet since that bloody night in July. The new perimeter of the Mohawk state was definitely secured. Sporadic gunshots could be heard, but these incidents were few and far between. Ill-advised and ill-equipped for the task, the RCMP was bitter about its defeat. They had good reason. The price in lives of their previous folly had been high.

Canada's finest now had two fronts to defend, the Mohawk state and the Free State of Quebec, and they were unable to throw their weight around with the abandon they had previously exhibited. The death of Dupré had sent the country into political turmoil, and higher leadership was almost nonexistent. Under such circumstances there was little the RCMP and armed forces could do but act as border guards. While Canada tried to hold herself together with chewing gum and baling wire at the high governmental level, the lower levels functioned as best they could without, they hoped, drawing the attention of that erratic group in Parliament. The less they interfered, the less chance of further mistakes or additional loss of lives.

The Nishnabe were fully aware of this sad situation in the north and with little physical threat so far from the U.S. side, despite the troop build-up, Akwesasne had become quite a different place. The traditional government had its feet well planted and the council ran as it had for seven hundred years, with few hitches beyond those that had always existed. It had, all things considered, been a beautiful summer.

On this fine, cool afternoon, the early autumn sun warmed the earth with tender care. A wave of new excitement flowed over the land. Hints of a diplomatic coup were carried on the soft fall breeze and a sudden tingle ran throughout the countryside. The winds whispered of new treaties.

Earlier in the month, the French government had signed a pact with the Free State of Quebec. Since France had supported the Free French Movement from the outset, this hadn't come as a complete surprise, not even to Canada. But now a three-way agreement was persistently rumored: a mutual defense pact between Quebec, France and Anishinabe-waki. The prospect of this new alliance created a stir among the nations of the world. It wouldn't put France in total agreement with the Communist Bloc, but it would bring into the open the anti–U.S. sentiment which had been simmering beneath the surface since the years of deGaulle. France's influence was stronger than the U.S. would have liked everyone to believe and now an alignment seemed to be forming which could be quite difficult to handle.

France would probably bring with her the support of four other European countries, the idea of which set official teeth on edge in Washington. About the only government still neutral was Switzerland. They, of course, managed to avoid becoming involved in the messy business of defending either side. They simply offered their services as mediator if requested.

Pawing the earth like a mad bull, the United States raged away in the UN, only to receive one rebuff after another. Its position was fast falling apart in this international body. The American ambassador could only take delaying action while Washington pulled together its trampled ego. International feelings running against the U.S. were now almost unbearable in weight as well as number. The State Department was also reduced to stalling tactics while the White House figured out a strategy which, when revealed, would put a sudden and complete halt to this rout. At least, that's what everyone hoped.

But for Jesse Hood, an Akwesasne Mohawk, events in Washington couldn't have seemed more distant. His summer had been one he would never forget. He was Nishnabe, a free man at last in his own country. He had a reason to live, even if it cost him his life in the long run. He hoped it would not, but some of his brothers had already paid that price and he was equally prepared.

A natural-born leader from a family with a strong warrior tradition, he had advanced rapidly in the Akwesasne forces and now commanded two hundred men. He had the military experience he needed. He had served in the elite Marine Reconnaissance Corps and distinguished himself behind enemy lines in Cambodia when he was only nineteen. Though he had often been sickened by it, that experience was now paying off in a meaningful way. He had come home from Southeast Asia with an empty feeling. Now he had a purpose. His four years had not been as wasted or as futile as he had previously believed.

Jesse's position sat well on his broad shoulders and he was liked by his troops. Little escaped his eyes. He knew each man by name, though many were newcomers who were not Mohawk. Twelve eastern Indian nations were represented in his command, from Tuscarora to Shawnee, Penobscot to eastern Cherokee. From the lightest-skinned to the darkest full-blood, all were Nishnabe. He even had a few of the new "White Mohawk" warriors and all were as one. The only "roll" here was roll call, and that only when necessary. Each man was simply expected to carry out his assignment in support of his war chief and his fellow Nishnabe. Each man did. Each knew the survival of his nation depended on it.

Finally official word came. The council had indeed signed a mutual defense pact with Quebec and France! Another was now under negotiation with Mexico, whose president just happened to be an Indian. In his communications, he alluded to what his predecessor, the "famous little Indian, Juarez" would have wanted for his brothers to the north. Zap!—another vocal arrow had struck the White House. Did the president have bad dreams? No one knew for sure. But he certainly had a constant headache!

"Hey, Jesse!"

"Little Brother." Jesse eased himself down against a tree in the warm sun.

"What you think about the treaty?"

"Good news, Little Brother, if this one is any good. Been a lot of treaties."

"Jesse, you're too damn hard sometimes."

"Nope, just want to see what they really do. 'Course it gives us a bit more weight and that can't hurt. Just wonder what it'll cost, that's all."

"What do you think it'll cost?"

"In our present position? Couldn't cost much. . . . There's not much for them to take."

"You know something I don't, Big Brother?"

"Probably a lot you don't, Tommy, but not about the treaty. Just remembering all the others. Not a pleasant thing to base a judgment on, as I recall. Just takes awhile to see it all. Sorta like those iceberg things —might just be the tip showing. All things considered, I'm sure it'll help now anyway . . . especially that one they're working on with Mexico. Too close for the U.S. not to feel the heat."

"Yeah! I'll bet Washington is full of messy pants right now. 'Specially in that big *White* House!" He laughed. "What I wouldn't give to be a mouse in that place right now. All those bigshots running into each other trying to shuffle enough paper to keep the boogeyman away. Eh-ah-h-h! Beautiful, man! Beautiful!"

"Easy, Little Brother, don't underestimate those big-shots. They may be paper-shufflers but they aren't stupid. Best you not let our small army go to your head just yet. One misjudgment on their part and they could just nuke us right off the face of the earth."

"Nuke us? Are you kidding?" Tommy hadn't considered that.

"Wish I was, but let's not forget what they've done before. They never had any qualms when it came to fighting redskins. They tried everything they could think of from smallpox to buying scalps. What's a little local nuke going to hurt? They got the stuff to do it."

"You think they really would?"

"I think they'll think about it. They thought about it in Asia; they'll think about it here. What they do is something else . . . . Your guess is as good as mine."

"Jesse, you scare the hell outta me!"

"Tommy, it scares the hell outta *me*, but all things must be considered. World opinion would be against it but if the U.S. is pushed far enough, it may decide to chuck world opinion. Then it wouldn't be unlikely at all. Just poof! No more Nishnabe! Easy as loading an M–16 . . . . Just poof!"

"Guess it could happen . . . . " Tommy's eyes had a faraway look.

"Sorry, Little Brother, but it damn well could." Jesse got up. "Soon as you come back, we'll get some coffee and see what we can find out about Mexico."

"Yeah."

White House War Room—Washington, D.C.
. . . August 28, 1976—7:38 P.M.

Charges. Countercharges. Recess. Recall. More
charges. Complaints about the UN Security Force.
The U.S. ambassador to the UN was doing his best to
bait the wolves, to buy time. To his dismay he was
unable to halt the pacts made between Anishinabe-
waki and France and Mexico. Equipment made in the
U.S. was once again pointed toward home, side by side
with a fair supply of Russian and Chinese armaments.
Threats flew like geese in the fall, only to be met by
counterthreats from one side or the other. If words
could kill, the UN would have been full of cadavers.
Tension grew, then slackened, only to be reinforced
with some new development, some new threat or new
deal.

Well aware of its waning strength in this international body, the White House was using it only to keep
in touch. It had become clear that if anything were to
be done, the United States would be facing the heavy

onslaught of most of the world powers. Her action, if taken in any form of overt act against the new nation, would meet with armed opposition from around the world. Knowing this, the president had embarked on a course of no return—no return as far as he knew.

The White House War Room was in a fever of activity. Plans were laid only to be washed for new ones which complied with the constantly changing face of things.

"Nuke 'em, by God, that's what I say! Nuke all them bastards!" General Tucker Sherman paced the floor.

"Nuke all what bastards?" the president asked, not looking up from a mass of reports he was studying.

"All of them—them Indians, the French, Mexico— all of 'em. Russia and China won't get into it! They got too much to lose! Just clean out those ratholes once and for all. Like I told you before, Mr. President, in fifteen minutes—just fifteen minutes—we could blow 'em all to their goddamn happy hunting grounds, or wherever the bastards go." He puffed heavily on his half-spent cigar. Col. Hal Jackson stood a few feet behind him, looking at the floor to keep his anger from showing. He had made up his mind to resign when this was all over. The general was making it harder and harder to hold on that long. But he knew that under the present circumstances he was trapped.

"General." The president hadn't yet looked up. "In part, I'm now inclined to agree with you. However, you are forgetting the ties many of our citizens have with France. After all, it's not like dropping H-bombs on Japs or Indians. The French are church-going white folk like us. I'm afraid it wouldn't set well here at home." Jackson bit his lip. "Besides, France has nuclear weapons and says she'll use 'em. You read that statement they made in the UN.

"No, General, we must use discretion. Perhaps localized nuclear weapons against the Indians and conventional bombs on the French . . . if that becomes necessary. That way we keep the people here at home from getting as upset as they would if we did indeed nuke Paris. I don't think they would mind if we dropped a dirty one on Peking though . . . . " Then he added with a smirk, " . . . almost like Japs . . . . Either way, France is into this with both feet and we have to stop her."

Col. Jackson spoke softly. "Mr. President, those Indians are human beings. You're talking about genocide, not to mention a third world war. Contrary to what seems to be the majority opinion, I don't think Russia and China will let this happen, nor will France and her allies . . . . And what about Congress, sir? We can't declare war on everyone without congressional approval and a formal declaration of war. Sir, this is not the Jacksonian Era!"

The president looked up. He eased forward in his chair.

"Colonel Jackson, let me remind you: *I* am the president. Congress can do what it will, but I am the president! Do I make myself clear?"

"Yes, sir, very . . . . " Jackson looked at the floor; his lip was catching hell.

"General."

"Mr. President?"

"How many aircraft armed with conventional bombs can we put over Paris?"

"Enough. I'd say thirty."

"Fine." The president reshuffled his papers and made a few notes. "And how long would it take to set up the three Indian states for limited nuclear weapons?"

"It's done."

"Done?"

"Yes, Mr. President, standard procedure."

"Just as well, it will save time." He made another note. "We don't want them to have time to use those Minutemen." He swiveled his chair to face the vice-president, who was sitting quietly to one side.

"Thad, I want you to meet with our people in the House and Senate. Feel it out. Find out where we can go if we ask for a declaration of war. Their determination will dictate our final preparation and action. Impress upon them that our backs are to the wall and we've no other choice. Don't mention the nuclear option." He glanced at Jackson. "You, Colonel, shall accompany Mr. Browning. I trust he may need your support from the military end. I know he will get it."

"Yes, Mr. President." Jackson's lip was bleeding on the inside. He hadn't registered the pain.

Senate Office Building—Washington, D.C.
. . . August 29, 1976—1:48 A.M.

"Colonel Jackson." Senator Dillman sat down hard in his large black leather chair, spilling scotch on his trousers. "Uh!" He adjusted his large bulk and took a pull on the extra-large glass. "Colonel, I won't ask you if this is important. I'll simply say that it had better be. I'm an old man and I need my rest."

"Is World War III important, Senator?"

Dillman set down his drink. "He's going to do it?"

"Looks that way."

"When?"

"I'd say within the next forty-eight hours."

"Jackson, man, are you certain?"

"Too certain to sleep! Too damn certain."

"Without Congress?"

"With or without. He's working on that now with his partisan group . . . but he intends to do it come hell or high water. That pact with Mexico was all he could stand. Too close to home."

"Yeah, that was a nasty cut. I was afraid it might push him into a corner. Appears it did."

The long silence was interrupted only by the clinking of ice. Thirty-eight years of public service lined the walls of the senator's office—pictures, plaques, and other mementos of a colorful political career. One small case held the picture of a young man in a marine uniform. It also contained two Purple Hearts, a Silver Star, two Bronze Stars, and various lesser medals. A bronze plaque read, "Corporal Thomas Carlman Dillman, U.S. Marine Corps. Killed in Action. Korea—August 15, 1952." He had been the senator's only son. He had lived seventeen years, eight months, five days.

"Goddamn war," the senator said softly, "and God damn those who make it."

Jackson's tired eyes looked up. "Ditto." He drained his glass. "... and screw the president of the United States!"

"Son, if someone heard that it might be called treason ... if someone heard it." The senator finished his drink.

Consulate of India, New York City
. . . August 29, 1976—8:55 A.M.

An Indian in a crisp white jacket brought a tray of coffee into the long room and placed a cup at each chair around the oblong conference table. Roy Bear Walks Backward and Ed Small Wolf stood in the morning sunshine at the tall windows that lined the end of the room. They spoke in low voices. Other members of the Anishinabe-waki Executive Council were drifting in, and, with a nod to the white man sitting at the end of the table, took their seats. Behind the white man's ruddy complexion sat tired but alert eyes. Alongside his coffee cup was a large glass of scotch and water.

Roy and Ed broke up their private talk and took their seats beside the huge bulk sipping the scotch.

"Gentlemen of the council, I wish you to say good morning to Senator Keller Dillman of Maine." Roy sat down. He looked up as the door opened and Hal Jackson entered. "Oh yes, and this is Colonel Hal Jackson, United States Army. The enemy," Roy grinned, "and AWOL, I believe."

"That, sir," Hal said with a timid smile, "is a matter for debate at the moment." He slid into an empty chair, facing Ed. *Hau Kola, Lakota.*"

"Ah! You speak our language." Ed was grinning. "*Hau Kola*, yourself. Aren't you afraid you'll tempt us heathens with that prize scalp of yours?"

"O.K. I could have stayed in Washington and been insulted!"

"Anybody can be insulted in Washington." Dillman said dryly. "The whole District is an insult!"

A chuckle went around the small group. It was followed by a few minutes of friendly chatter and the rattle of coffee cups. Finally Roy stood, called them to order, and laid out what he and Dillman along with Jackson and Small Wolf had discussed in the two hours preceding the meeting.

"Gentlemen," he concluded, "I have little need to tell you our time is short. We have asked to meet with the American ambassador to the UN at one o'clock this afternoon, assuming of course the president holds off that long. We are all aware of the time factor involved and the decision that must be made. It could be our last."

Dillman spoke up. "Gentlemen, for nearly forty years I've served my country. I want you to be fully aware that my country is still foremost in my mind and heart. Don't misunderstand my reasons for coming here. I wish only to avoid unnecessary killing on both sides. My people in Washington have been working toward that end most of the early morning. However, considering the planning capabilities of the White House, we must act and act quickly to avoid such a horrible mistake. The situation is beyond critical, not only for our two countries, but for the world. The time is short and getting shorter. Canada has already shown us the results of rash action. Japan still recalls the blunder it made at Pearl Harbor. Any such misjudgment now on your part or on the part of the president could spell the end to both Anishinabe-waki and the United States." Dillman took a long pull on his scotch. "You have come too far to go back, but I remind you, the twilight of the gods waits just beyond the hill. One miscalculation and we'll all be sitting in rubble up to our ears.

"Weigh your possibilities carefully. Consider your information and may God help all of you. The colonel and I shall wait at the UN for word of your plan."

United Nations—New York City
... August 29, 1976—12:45 P.M.

With an escort of two Nishnabe troopers, Ed Small Wolf approached the suite of the American ambassador to the UN. Ed entered the well-appointed office with a rock in the pit of his stomach. The hastily thrown together proposal he carried was not, in his opinion, in the best interest of the Nishnabe, but if accepted it could stop the rash action of the president and give everyone involved a way out with little loss of face. More important, it would stop World War III.

Small Wolf had been chosen to deal directly with the president through Senator Dillman. Some opposition to this had come up in the council, but was quickly overcome when it was stressed that Small Wolf had experience in Washington that no one else on the Executive Council could boast. He had dealt with the president before and would know what to expect from him. If necessary, he could change tactics and still come up standing on his feet—a neat trick by any standards.

Dillman, sitting in a low, comfortable chair with his ever-present glass, didn't rise when Ed came in. The ambassador did and offered his most formal self to the young Nishnabe.

"Mr. Small Wolf, I believe?"

"You believe correctly, sir." He nodded to Dillman. "Senator."

Dillman returned the nod. "Congressman."

"Just *Mr.* Small Wolf, Senator."

"Mr. Small Wolf." Dillman grinned and took a pull at his glass. "I've heard stories about Indian Time but you're fifteen minutes early."

"Perhaps Indian Time is now, Senator."

"Perhaps, Mr. Small Wolf, perhaps." Dillman settled deeper in his chair. "Let us hope it isn't time to go bang." His voice carried no humor.

Ed was offered a chair and seated himself.

"Have you heard from Washington, Senator?" Ed didn't like Dillman's choice of words.

"I've heard enough to know we're fighting uphill all the way, and I do mean all the way, Mr. Small Wolf."

"The president's gaining support?"

"Ed, the president *is* all the support he needs. From his point of view, the rest is just window-dressing. But then that pact with Mexico has assured him some votes in Congress. Too damn many were pressed into panic. With no control to speak of in Canada, this threat from the south shook a lot of people up. Now we have two unstable borders. That's a bit unsettling.

Not to mention the borders of Anishinabe-waki . . . . "
Ed agreed.

"Where's Hal?"

"Had to get back. General needs a whipping boy. Besides, Hal feels he can do more good in close like that. Sherman could be a stumbling block for any compromise offer we might come up with."

It was obvious that the honorable ambassador to the United Nations was more than a little mystified by the undiplomatic way in which these two men were dealing. He had expected a stand-off, but now he couldn't even tell that they were on different sides. Deciding he had been wolf-bait in formal circles for long enough, he simply settled back to listen. The senator set his glass down and lit a cigarette, offering one to Ed.

"Now, what did the Executive Council come up with? Hmmm?"

Ed took the cigarette, a habit he had only recently acquired, then pulled a folder from the briefcase at his side.

"Not sure this will get the job done, but it's as far as we will go—too damn far, in my opinion." He began reading from the text.

> "Article I: The United States of America shall recognize the Anishinabe-waki democracy as an independent and sovereign nation with all rights and privileges accorded to such nations and its representatives.

"Article II: Anishinabe-waki will not attempt to expand its present borders, except insofar as to claim adjoining land heretofore unlawfully annexed by the United States in violation of its treaties with sovereign Indian nations. It will hold such lands in trust in the name of those nations in accordance with previous treaties.

"Article III: Anishinabe-waki will return all citizens of the United States now held within its borders and make arrangements for settlement with civilians who wish to stay, under the terms of the Anishinabe Democracy.

"Article IV: Anishinabe-waki will enter into negotiations with the United States of America to settle all claims to land and monies due Indian nations now part of Anishinabe-waki under those treaties which the United States has failed to honor; all payments due will be rendered at present rates of exchange plus all accrued interest.

"Article V: The governments of Anishinabe-waki and the United States of America will enter into negotiations aimed at the development of a mutual nonaggression treaty.

"Article VI: The United States of America will recognize the right of Anishinabe-waki to act as representative for any Indian nation outside its territorial boundaries if so requested by said nation, in any dealings with the United States by said Indian nation.

"Article VII: Upon acceptance of this agreement all military forces will be withdrawn from the borders of Anishinabe-waki and all hostilities shall cease between these two nations.

"This is signed by the head of our Executive Council, Roy Bear Walks Backward." Ed took a drink offered by the ambassador's secretary. After a long pull, he set down the glass and continued.

"This agreement, Senator, is accompanied by a four-page supplement which covers various other subtopics and items of contention, such as grants made by kings, the Doctrine of Divine Right in Discovery, etcetera. Well?"

"Well, hell, when you've only got one bullet, you do the best you can with the first shot. I suggest we get moving. Mr. Ambassador, will you contact the White House and request a meeting?"

Shocked by the simplicity of the entire affair, it was with great effort that the ambassador held the tone of the meeting. He made the necessary arrangements but failed miserably to be simple and straightforward. He'd been a diplomat too long.

Oval Office of the President—Washington, D.C.
... August 29, 1976—7:51 P.M.

The president entered his office in his usual confident manner and gave a brief smile to the two men who stood at his entrance.

"Senator ... Mr. Small Wolf, good evening." With him was Vice-President Browning, General Sherman, and Colonel Jackson. A small group of aides brought up the rear. "Please have a seat."

Along with the secretaries of state and defense, the president had studied copies of the Anishinabe-waki agreement sent by special military courier. He looked resolute, but a hint of fatigue appeared around his eyes and mouth and he had his usual headache. He took some aspirins from a desk drawer and downed them with a glass of water from his desk service. He appeared to relax a bit as he sat down.

"Coffee, please, and whatever these gentlemen wish; scotch for the senator .... Mr. Small Wolf?"

"Scotch ... please."

"Well, gentlemen, it's been a busy day for all of us, eh?"

"Not one I'd like to repeat at my age." Senator Dillman tested his drink.

"Nor I," said the president. He really meant it. "Mr. Small Wolf, how are you holding up?"

"A bit tired, Mr. President."

"Yes, I imagine we could all use a rest."

Ed couldn't quite figure out all this small talk. The men who had come in with the president were as tight as catgut on a violin, but the president seemed to be more relaxed all the time. He was even smiling off and on. Ed sensed that someone wasn't quite in tune.

"Mr. Small Wolf." The president leaned forward. "I believe it's time to present our decision on your proposed disengagement measures."

General Sherman smiled. Small Wolf knew Sherman; his smile made Ed's stomach tighten. He glanced at Hal Jackson, who had a numb look on his face.

"My people eagerly await your word, sir."

"The orders are issued, Mr. Small Wolf. The United States of America can no longer accept the threat which your people have placed within our nation . . . ."

"Your nation! This land was ours! We're asking for nothing but to keep what we have left!" For a brief instant, Ed once again saw the line of blue-coats and could taste dust in his throat. A war cry sounded in his head. He was on his feet as a Secret Service agent came through the door. Senator Dillman glanced at the floor, a deep sadness in his eyes.

"Mr. Small Wolf, as president of the United States and commander in chief of the armed forces, I hereby demand the immediate and unconditional surrender of the nation of Anishinabe-waki."

Ed sat down, his face frozen in an icy glare. Dillman offered him a cigarette.

"I'm sorry, son, very sorry."

Ed took the smoke and slowly lit it. His eyes never left the face of the president. "So am I, Senator. We only wanted peace. Now we are forced to react as your people have taught us." Ed looked at his watch.

"Mr. President, it is now eight-fourteen P.M. In less than an hour, three of your own missiles will be launched. They are targeted on Washington, D.C. We do not wish to destroy innocent people but we have been pushed to our limit—this is where the sun stops. The war lance is at your throat."

A shock ran through the room.

Trying to control his expression, the president spoke slowly. "Mr. Small Wolf, your bluff will not work. You are an intelligent man and you are also sitting in the so-called target area."

"My spirit does not wish to go to the Outer World, Mr. President. You're right; I, too, will die. But I am of a warrior tradition and I'm prepared to die for my people. Aren't you?"

"General, order evacuation . . . "

"Excuse me, Mr. President," Colonel Jackson broke

in. "If what Ed says is true, there is no way we could beat those missiles. From launch to target . . . well, we hardly have time for a quick drink."

"Quick drink, hell! What about our high-priced anti-missile system?" The president was halfway out of his chair.

"Mr. President." In spite of his faults, Sherman had courage. "Our anti-missile system is not programmed for our own missiles. If it was, it would blow up our missiles before they got out of the country!"

Dillman had a sad grin on his face. "In that case, let's have one for the road."

His features almost gray, the president leaned back. "Sherman, are you absolutely certain?"

"Yes, Mr. President, I'm afraid I am."

"Well, Mr. Small Wolf, how long have we got?"

"Not much more than an hour."

"Well, gentlemen, our government will be totally destroyed. A president must expect to give his life for his country but I do not believe that I have the right to sit by while our entire nation is ruined." He asked for a drink and took a long pull at it. "Mr. Small Wolf, can you prevent the firing of those missiles?"

"Yes, if we don't waste any more time."

"I do not know if you are bluffing or not, Small Wolf, but I do know you are a brave man. Sherman, issue the recall, *now!*"

Senator Dillman was enjoying his scotch and looking forward to the next, the one he thought he'd never get to drink.

"Mr. Small Wolf, send your message. Then we'll make arrangements for high-level talks with your government."

"Thank you, Mr. President." Ed barely repressed a triumphant smile as he rose to leave. The bluff had worked.

Senator Dillman sat back and sipped his scotch. He had seen the smile in Ed's eyes. Now he knew what he had suspected all along: The warheads had been dismantled before the bargaining had begun. Dillman had been around long enough to know that the Indian people had never played doomsday games but he doubted that the president would understand or appreciate that.

Capitol Building—Washington, D.C.
. . . September 5, 1976—1:15 P.M.

The crew scurried around, dodging booms, wires, cables, and cameras as they moved into position. The headsets of the cameramen crackled with orders. "Stand-by one . . . two on the seal." Television sets all over the United States lit up.

"Ladies and Gentlemen . . . the President of the United States . . . . "

"Two . . . fade out. Now one."

The president's well-groomed and rested person appeared on the screens of sixty million television sets across the country.

"My fellow Americans," he began in a strong voice —the birthday party was on again! And with it the birth of a new nation. The president knew how to handle both to his advantage.

Cabolclo . . . September 5, 1976—Late evening

Later, much later . . . in the state of Cabolclo, Ani-shinabe-waki Democracy, a victory dance was in progress. The songs that were sung were older than the plains themselves. Tall figures danced around the large fire in the middle of the agency center. New songs were sung, made up on the spur of the moment. It was a happy time.

Off to one side, two men surveyed the happy scene before them—Emil Tall Warrior and Art Navarro.

The drums had slowed to the rhythm of an Honor Dance. Eight and nine abreast, the dancers slowly moved clockwise around the fire, their feet in time to the thunder drum. Leading them was a lone figure, the girl called Twila. Her lovely head was held high, silent tears glistening on her cheeks. Her shawl swayed quietly, her white buckskin dress, leggings, and moccasins showed yellow, red, and gold in the firelight. Across her arms, held close to her breast, she carried a surplus AR–15 with a new eagle feather hanging from the barrel.

A light breeze blew out of the north, cooling the land. The Indians' summer was over. Far off in an eastern forest a hawk cried. It was the time of the People.

Paka
(Beautiful)